Killer Punch

By Amy Korman

KILLER PUNCH
KILLER GETAWAY
KILLER WASPS

Killer Punch

A Killer WASPs Mystery

AMY KORMAN

WITNESS
IMPULSE
An Imprint of HarperCollinsPublishers

KILLER PUNCH. Copyright © 2016 by Amy Korman. All rights reserved under International and Pan-American Copyright Conventions. By payment of the required fees, you have been granted the nonexclusive, nontransferable right to access and read the text of this e-book on screen. No part of this text may be reproduced, transmitted, downloaded, decompiled, reverse-engineered, or stored in or introduced into any information storage and retrieval system, in any form or by any means, whether electronic or mechanical, now known or hereafter invented, without the express written permission of HarperCollins e-books. For information, address HarperCollins Publishers, 195 Broadway, New York, NY 10007.

EPub Edition AUGUST 2016 ISBN: 9780062431134
Print Edition ISBN: 9780062431318

10 9 8 7 6 5 4 3 2 1

Killer Punch

Chapter 1

I was painting the walls of my antiques store, The Striped Awning, when Sophie Shields showed up with a Venti mocha in one hand and a sheaf of legal papers in the other.

"Barclay and I are, like, three weeks away from getting our divorce done, if I can just get my Giuseppe Zanottis back," Sophie Shields told me, parking her tiny tush on my in-the-manner-of-Chippendale desk chair, and pushing up a pair of huge sunglasses on top of her blond hair. "I'm missing seventeen pairs of shoes, and I happen to know that my ex has a thing for strappy sandals!"

Sophie is four-eleven, with huge brown eyes, a sweetly upbeat personality, and—despite her small stature—a surprisingly steely core, which she attributes to having lived in New Jersey until a couple of years ago. Apparently, if you can survive being married to former mid-level mafia exec Barclay Shields and have driven the Turnpike and the Garden State Parkway on a regular basis, you're ready for anything.

I put down my paintbrush and gratefully accepted the huge coffee. It was a sunny, breezy Thursday in July in Bryn Mawr, our little town outside Philadelphia, and I was kicking off the summer antiques season at my shop—where, to be honest, there is no summer season. Sales had been really slow recently, so I'd gone to the hardware store on Sunday and picked up three gallons of Smashing Pink paint, which I was currently rolling onto the walls of the shop using an old broom handle and a four-dollar roller brush.

This fuchsia color would definitely lure in foot traffic!

Er . . . probably it would. At least that's what I'd thought over the weekend. The hot-pink paint was turning out to be a little more of an eyeful than I'd thought, but I was determined to finish the paint job—even though, eight hours in, I hadn't completely covered even one wall yet. The paint was so bright that even a single streak needed to be corrected immediately. I sighed, gulped some mocha—maybe not the best idea at five in the afternoon—and headed toward the back of the store where my hated paint roller awaited.

"I thought you and Barclay were still arguing over the Versace plates and the time-share in Vegas," I said to Sophie, picking up the roller and climbing back onto my stepladder as Waffles, my portly and good-natured basset hound, came over to Sophie and sat wagging and drooling at her feet.

"You're right!" said Sophie, giving Waffles a timid pat on his head. "I'm pissed about the plates. But a guy who's got a closetful of size five and a half women's shoes—that's just creepy! 'Cause Barclay wears a men's thirteen! Not that I think he's trying to *wear* my sandals, exactly. But my personal trainer Gerda once told me that she caught my ex in bed with all my shoes piled around him, including a Gucci platform number he was about to buckle onto his—"

Thankfully, Sophie's story was interrupted, because the door to the shop was flung open by Bootsie McElvoy.

"I'm back from the L.L. Bean warehouse sale in Maine, and I

scored BIG," Bootsie told us, gesturing to her Range Rover, which was illegally parked out front with two kayaks strapped to the top. Sophie and I emerged onto the sidewalk to admire Bootsie's haul: Her car was indeed absolutely stuffed, with tents and foldable lounge chairs filling the trunk and backseat, and a paddleboard sticking out of the passenger side back window.

"I hit the sale at 8 a.m., and left Freeport right after I shopped and got the car packed." She inspected her watch. "Only took me six hours and fifty-five minutes to get back here, *and* I stopped at the Progresso warehouse in Jersey, Kristin. Got you a case of slightly damaged soup at half price."

Here, Bootsie indicated a cardboard box in the front seat filled with dented cans of tomato-basil and minestrone. I was touched, honestly. Bootsie knows my budget constraints and lack of culinary skill mean that soup is my main source of nutrition.

"Thanks so much!" I said, giving her a hug.

"What's that blue thingy next to the soup?" asked Sophie.

"It's a packable sink," Bootsie said, as if this was obvious. She opened the passenger door, reached in, pulled on a Velcro strap, and the nylon popped into a large giant basin shape. "For camping. Marked down to seven-fifty from forty-two bucks."

Sophie looked doubtful. "I once got two Fendi Baguettes for half off at a sample sale, but ya got me beat on discount shopping!" she told Bootsie. "Although what you're gonna do with a pop-up sink, I don't know."

I've known Bootsie since we attended Bryn Mawr Prep fifteen years ago together, along with our closest friends Holly Jones and Joe Delafield, and I know for a fact that she actually uses all this camping equipment. Also, Bootsie loves a good road trip, during which she blasts her Jimmy Buffet bootlegs.

"Haven't you ever gone camping?" Bootsie asked Sophie.

"I'm from Jersey," Sophie reminded Bootsie. "We don't do camping. But we *do* do drinks, and I could use a vodka if you girls are ready to hit the Pub!"

"Great!" I said. "Oh, wait, I promised myself I'd work on this redecorating project till seven tonight. You two go ahead," I added mournfully as Bootsie carried the case of soup into my shop.

"What's with the pink paint?" Bootsie asked me, eyeing the half-painted back wall critically.

"Business is kind of slow," I told her. "I'm thinking an attention-grabbing color will bring in business."

Bootsie opened her mouth to tell me everything that was wrong with my pink project, but as luck would have it, her phone dinged with an incoming text. Since Bootsie's addicted to technology, the text won out.

"There's an issue at the country club," Bootsie read from her screen. "Holly says it's urgent. We need to get there ASAP."

"How urgent?" I asked.

"Honey Potts brought in a painting last night as part of an art lecture she was planning to give at the party Saturday night," Bootsie said, "and now the painting's gone. It's, like, one hundred and fifty years old and is a rare work by Hasley Huntingdon-Mews, which means it's worth one hundred thousand dollars."

"Okay, that actually is urgent," I agreed, as Sophie's eyes widened with interest and she grabbed her purse, a vast gold leather Versace number that featured both fringe and studs.

Phew—a good excuse to take a break from my paint job! I thought, then experienced a faint stab of guilt, since Mrs. Potts was no doubt feeling devastated by the theft of her pricey artwork. Of course, Honey Potts is heiress to a vast old-money fortune, and lives on an estate somewhere north of three hundred and fifty acres, but it still had to hurt.

I went into the store's tiny bathroom, tried to remove the most egregious blobs of pink paint from my hair and arms, took off my Old Navy T-shirt and shorts, and threw on a striped Gap Outlet sundress that I keep there for emergencies. I brushed my hair, swiped on some mascara as I pondered the unlikely painting theft.

Things had been hectic all week at the club, where setup was under way for Saturday's preview bash for the Bryn Mawr Tomato Show, a two-part event held in July every year. It's hard to overstate the importance of the Tomato Show in our little town. I mean, not that Sophie or I know a Mr. Stripey from a San Marzano, but tons of people around Bryn Mawr are obsessed by cultivating the delicate veggie, including Bootsie's mom, Kitty Delaney.

In country-club terms, a stolen painting in the middle of the Tomato Show setup counted as a Major Fuckup. I gave Waffles a refill of water and a Milk-Bone, then locked up, trying to ignore his droopy, soulful expression at being left at the store for an hour.

"Anyway, what The Striped Awning needs isn't pink paint. This store is crying out for a specialty cocktail," Bootsie told me, gesturing dismissively around my tiny store as I locked the door behind us and we climbed into her Range Rover, Sophie in the front with the pop-up sink, while I wedged myself in the back with the paddleboard. "Booze brings in foot traffic."

"Bootsie, it's an antiques store, not T.G.I. Friday's," I told her. "I'm trying to sell silver serving trays, not Strawberry 'Ritas."

"That's where you're wrong," Bootsie told me airily. "Free alcohol is exactly what this place needs. As soon as I solve this painting problem, I'll figure out your store's signature drink!"

Chapter 2

Bootsie took the turn into the country club on two wheels, then came to a sudden halt behind a jam-up of trucks in the club's driveway.

Right in front of us, guys in shorts and T-shirts were unloading low white sofas from The Trendy Tent, a company that supplies high-end party settings. The Trendy Tent charges hefty fees for the use of rental furniture that I'm pretty sure would be cheaper to buy right from IKEA. My rich friend Holly Jones always hires them for parties, then adds gorgeous details like walkways lined by twenty-foot-tall flowering magnolia trees in January and seven-arm chandeliers created entirely of orange blossoms.

More workmen were carrying enormous Lucite coffee tables around the corner of the clubhouse, and just down the driveway, I could see a huge white truck with a familiar dark green logo in fancy script: "Colkett Interior and Landscape Design: A Lifestyle Transformation!"

"The Colketts are back from Los Angeles!" shrieked Sophie. "Perfect timing, 'cause I want to get my backyard ready for when

Joe and I tie the knot. I've got a whole Pinterest board ready. It's gonna be Kim and Kanye meet Ina Garten, with an extra-large dose of Vegas sizzle that I'll sneak in when Joe isn't looking!"

"I can't wait!" I told Sophie encouragingly.

The truth is that Sophie's boyfriend, Joe Delafield, is a professional interior designer and is adamantly anti-glitter, gilt, and anything gilded or encrusted with Swarovski crystals—all of which Sophie loves. There's no way Joe—who's been honing his signature antiques-mixed-with-modern decor mantra since the age of fifteen, when he gave the student lounge at our prep school a stylish new look—would let anything close to casino-style glitz near their wedding.

If there *is* a wedding, that is: Sophie's divorce from Barclay has been more than a year in the making and is always getting bogged down by legal filings about things like what night each gets Table 11 at Ristorante Gianni, our town's best restaurant. Joe probably doesn't need to start picking out a wedding song yet.

Actually, Barclay was the reason that Bootsie, Joe, and I had all met Sophie. A little over a year ago, Barclay—a former mafia exec, now a zealous developer of townhomes—had been whacked on the head and stashed under a hydrangea bush across the street from my house. Sophie and Barclay had already been mid-divorce when he'd gotten knocked out last spring, and she'd stopped by The Striped Awning after I'd had the bad luck to stumble on Barclay's prone form.

As things worked out, Sophie soon fell madly in love with Joe— great news, in my opinion, since Sophie has a huge heart under her flashy exterior. I'd spent a week in Florida with them over the winter, along with our friend Holly, who was co-chairing Saturday night's Tomato Party, and they seemed truly happy together.

At the moment, Joe was back in Florida finishing up a kitchen "installation," as he insists on calling it. (Translation: The client had him arranging her dishtowels.)

"And maybe the Colketts can plant that dumb vegetable patch Joe wants," Sophie continued. "Joe doesn't garden! But he says we should install, like, four thousand spinach plants.

"Which reminds me of the time Barclay had to recover from getting his stomach stapled—which didn't work, by the way!—at Canyon Ranch. I came back from a hike and found my ex and two girls in the bathtub, naked except for spinach detox masks, and that spinach was ladled onto them *everywhere* . . . Hey, is that a margarita machine?" she finished, sticking her head out the window as Bootsie slowed her car.

A large stainless steel frozen drink dispenser was indeed being wheeled by on a dolly.

"That's so cool!" I said, excited.

I mean, who doesn't like a margarita machine? This had to have been Holly's idea. Holly seems too perfect to put on a fun party, since she is heiress to a poultry fortune and has sleek blond hair, almond-shaped blue eyes, and a closet full of twenty-two-hundred-dollar sundresses and caftans. However, the awesome thing about her is that just when you're thinking you're in for a horrible night filled with snails served on orchid flowers, she busts out an amazing idea.

"Can we focus, please?" Bootsie ordered, pulling over and parking on what had been a perfect patch of emerald lawn.

"Obviously, we're going to be first in line for the frozen drinks as soon as they plug that thing in," Bootsie added, turning off the engine and leaping from the driver seat. "You two track down Holly and find out everything she knows about this painting theft.

"Then," Bootsie said, "we get some drinks!"

With that, Bootsie was gone, legging it around a rose hedge toward the club porch. I wondered, not for the first time since I met her in ninth grade at Bryn Mawr Prep, if science might want to study Bootsie's genetic makeup.

How could she tear through a twenty-four-hour warehouse sale of canoes and Coleman stoves before dawn, then drive more than six hours, hit the Progresso soup factory, and not be tired? And, how the heck did she convince her husband, Will; her toddler sons; and her boss at the local paper, the *Bryn Mawr Gazette*, that she could disappear to places like Maine and Florida for days—sometimes weeks—and both stay married and employed?

"Tim and Tom!" shrieked Sophie, as two tall, handsome men in well-pressed khakis and dress shirts approached. "Mwah!" she added, making kissy noises in their direction. "You Colketts keep getting more gorgeous by the minute!"

"DOLLS!" SAID TIM, as both men gave me and Sophie huge hugs, as usual smelling like a magnificent forest crossed with a pleasant citrus scent. The Colketts, who started out as Bryn Mawr's premier landscapers and florists, have lately gone to the big time, since they helped design a restaurant in Magnolia Beach, Florida, last winter that got national attention. Last I'd heard, they'd been in California working on a swanky new eatery called Viale with celebrity chef Gianni Brunello. Gianni's another Bryn Mawr fixture who's recently become so in demand that he's now filming the first season of his Food Network show, *The Angry Chef*.

"How'd ya get time off from that restaurant project?" Sophie queried. "I thought you guys were, like, busting your balls on that place 24/7."

"We are," Tim Colkett assured her. "I haven't slept in forty-seven days! But since Gianni made the entire construction team work well over the legal limit of ninety-eight hours per week, we got picketed, and he had to give us a few days off. However, he ordered us to stay in our hotel in L.A., so we don't want him to know we're back here in Bryn Mawr."

"Gianni's super-cheap," agreed Tom. "Luckily, the Food Network isn't, so we have a great suite at the Beverly Wilshire. Anyway, we promised Holly months ago that we'd decorate this party for her!"

"We love Holly," his business partner, Tom, added. "I mean, she had us import twenty-seven Venetian chandeliers to hang from the sycamores tonight, and the shipping and rewiring alone cost nine thousand dollars! And naturally, Holly's underwriting the whole cost of this shindig."

I sighed. Three years ago, Holly married a wealthy garbage and trucking mogul—not that she needed more cash, since her dad owns poultry farms all over Pennsylvania, and an average year's earnings for the Purdue clan is chicken feed to him. A few pricey chandeliers won't dent her bank account. Still—nine thousand dollars on tree lights?

"Do either of you know anything about this missing painting?" I asked the Colketts.

"We heard a ruckus about it, but to be honest, I didn't really focus on it," whispered Tom. "I mean, cows in a painting? No, thanks! And even worse, Mrs. Potts was gonna give a *lecture* about it. It's so Dame Maggie Smith, and not in a good way."

"Seriously—snore fest!" echoed Tim. "Who's going to pause mid-party for a monologue about milking and mooing?"

I realized that per usual, the Colketts might have already

downed a few of their favorite cocktails, which (conveniently, given they were working with an all-tomato theme), are Bloody Marys.

"If I were you, I'd go check in with Holly," advised Tim. "She *looks* as perfect as ever, but I think her co-chair on this tomato throwdown has her about to crack. I mean, we get along with everybody, but Eula Morris is about as much fun as dental surgery."

I shuddered, nodding sympathetically. Actually, this was another reason I'd been avoiding Holly recently: *Eula Morris*. The head of the tomato contest for the past six years, Eula had been royally pissed off when Honey Potts had ordered her to add Holly as co-chair. Since Mrs. Potts runs every social and charitable event in our town, Eula had to suck it up and plaster a smile on her face, but I could tell it was killing her to have to work with Holly.

Eula was our nemesis in high school, and if anything, the last fifteen years had made her even more annoying. Holly herself absolutely loathes Eula, with whom she's clashed over everything from the theme of our senior prom to the lights on the town Christmas tree, and the fact that they were jointly running this event made me wonder just how many of the anxiety meds Holly keeps for emergencies she'd gulped in the past few days.

"Plus Eula's ideas are terrible," Tom seconded. "I mean, I get it, it's a tomato show, but of course Eula got stuck on the obvious and pushed for a Tuscan farm theme with red lanterns and tomato topiaries. Plus, like we told Eula, all that red wasn't doing her complexion any favors—she's spent way too much time on the tennis court, and she's super splotchy."

Tim nodded. "Meanwhile, we're bringing the L.A. to PA! Between the palm trees and movie stars out there, we're totally inspired. We've created half the tent in 1940s Hollywood Regency meets '70s Jack Nicholson, with the bar painted a glossy dark gray and a loungy, moody vibe that's totally un-tomato. Then, in the other half, we're installing white sofas and Lucite tables on floors painted a cool red-and-white chevron pattern. The only hint of tomato will be huge six-foot-tall glass vases filled with glossy red Romas. Trust me, unless you assemble seven thousand of them in a sculptural display and light them properly, there's nothing chic about nightshade vegetables."

"I think tomatoes are technically a berry, believe it or not," Tom told him.

"Whatever," said Tim. "Although Eula actually painted some still-lifes to hang in the party tent of, like, Beefsteaks on the vine! We hung them in a corner behind where the tomatoes are going to be staged, and luckily Eula got mad and demanded her paintings back. Phew! The point is, the party isn't really about the Big Boys and Sweet Seedless hybrids. It's about showing up in a great outfit and having some drinks! Seriously, what good is a tomato unless it's turned into juice, blended with vodka, and spiked with horseradish and a big old stick of celery?"

Since this question didn't seem to really demand an answer, we exchanged good-byes and Sophie made some more smooch air kisses with the guys.

I noticed that the club was looking extra beautiful this afternoon. To be honest, when Holly's in party-planning mode, it's a good time to avoid her, and I hadn't stopped over for almost a week. During my absence, huge pink roses had burst into bloom all around the clubhouse, and banks of lilies wafted a magnificent fragrance over the shady grounds. Huge sycamores cast graceful shadows in the late-afternoon sun, and I breathed the non-paint-fumed air gratefully.

I followed Sophie through the huge wooden front doors into the rambling old clubhouse, where just outside the cozy bar area, there was Holly.

Holly was directing the placement of some potted fruit trees on the porch, looking serene in a chic white sleeveless dress and flat brown sandals, her long blond hair as glossy and effortless as ever. If you don't know Holly, she can be a little intimidating: She's one of those naturally flawless girls who is somehow always glows with a light tan, sleek hair, and some simple but pricey outfit that costs more than The Striped Awning brings in during an average month. However, Holly's the most loyal friend imaginable, and she's all about sharing her good fortune, including her wardrobe.

Holly projected an air of calm as she talked to a shorter, stouter young woman in a swoopy beige dress—the aforementioned Eula Morris—but I knew she was seething inside. Eula's been a preppy thorn in Holly's side for more than fifteen years, ever since their senior prom theme clash (Holly's super-cool 1970s–Bianca Jagger–Studio 54 idea had won out in a class vote over Eula's *Grease*-inspired sock-hop concept).

As I heard Eula say, "I knew we should have spent some of that fourteen thousand dollars we're spending on flowers and hired a security guard," I suddenly recalled that Eula had once beaten Holly out in a campaign for junior class treasurer at Bryn Mawr Prep.

Since Holly is the kind of willowy blonde who wafts through life without ever losing to anyone, I knew neither one of them had forgotten. Maybe that's why Holly had agreed to co-chair this party, a decision I'd had trouble understanding.

"Eula, you just don't understand parties," Holly told her with a forced sweetness and a note of fake pity. "Having this painting stolen means the Tomato Show is already a huge success! People *love* crime with their cocktails. My intern Jared just told me he's gotten forty-five new ticket sales in the last twenty minutes!"

Holly paused for a second and regrouped. "Obviously, it's a huge tragedy for Mrs. Potts, who's basically the Brooke Astor of Bryn Mawr, so we need to get the painting back," she added, "but I'm going to help Officer Walt with that as soon as I help the Colketts figure out how many orchids go in each branch of the flowering light fixtures."

As much as I dislike Eula, I felt a pang of sympathy for her. Her neck was turning pink with rage, and her beige dress looked slightly rumpled next to Holly's pristine white cotton one. That's the thing about Holly—she just doesn't rumple. As her friend, I'm used to the fact that she wafts through life having drinks bought for her and getting upgraded to an even better first-class seat than the one she originally paid for. For Eula, though, it had to rankle. Plus Eula was wearing a necklace and earrings comprised of tiny red tomato charms that looked absolutely awful. Even with my Old Navy budget and lack of fashion mojo, I knew tomato jewelry was a risky idea.

It seemed like Holly had the situation well in hand, plus Eula scares me a little, so I took a left turn and said hi to Skipper Parnell, the club's preppy blond chef, who was out on the porch, admiring the gorgeous white canvas structure that The Trendy Tent had just finished erecting. Just then, Bootsie popped back in from the bar, where I could see Officer Walt, Bryn Mawr's sole policeman, in earnest conversation with Honey Potts.

Nearby lurked Jared, an eighteen-year-old recent graduate of Bryn Mawr Prep who interns with Officer Walt, and is also serving as Holly's part-time tomato assistant. Jared's a nice enough kid, but is lanky, uncoordinated, and has a huge crush on Holly and spends most of his time staring at her slack-jawed, which isn't a great look because he still has braces.

"Everyone needs to be in the Camellia Room," Bootsie yelled to anyone within shouting distance. "Walt's going to put this place on lockdown in a few minutes."

"Oh, hi, Bootsie," said Eula, giving her a breezy little wave. "I see you're back from your *vacation*."

She gave this last a snippy edge, to indicate that leaving town was an indulgence enjoyed only by irresponsible slackers—which is sometimes true in Bootsie's case, but then again, no one else in town is as annoyingly driven as Eula, who tirelessly raises funds for the Symphony Women's Board all winter, and spends summers perfecting her tomatoes and her tennis game.

"I've got great news," continued Eula. "I've joined the *Gazette* as part-time reporter. We'll *both* be covering the party and real estate beat!"

Bootsie froze, her mouth agape. A moment later, a stream of F-bombs flew out. "If you think for one freakin' minute that you're going to steal my stories," she told Eula, grabbing a silver tennis trophy from a nearby display case, "I'm gonna take this trophy, which by the way I've been awarded as women's singles champion for the last four summers, and shove it right up your— "

"We need everyone in the Camellia Room now!" boomed Mrs. Potts. "Pronto!"

TWO MINUTES LATER, inside the Camellia Room, which is used for club board meetings and the occasional bridge game, I took a surreptitious look at Mrs. Potts, who had to be upset about the theft of her artwork. She looked about the same as she always did:

tanned, fit, somewhere in her late sixties, makeup-free face, and in Bermuda shorts. I had to hand it to her: Mrs. Potts is one of those stalwart, indomitable ladies whose herd of cows is her main passion in life; stolen paintings don't rattle her. She comes from a long line of never-say-die Pottses, who've been doing things like fighting the British at the Battle of Valley Forge since time immemorial.

Fear and self-pity aren't really allowed in the Potts bloodline. One Potts survived the *Lusitania* by doing a swan dive and swimming to the shore of Ireland, and a battalion of Mrs. Potts's uncles and cousins stormed the beaches of Europe during World War II. They just don't give up.

"Should we cancel the party?" asked Eula. "Because I feel absolutely terrible for Mrs. Potts here." She gave Holly a nasty little glare. "Even if other people want to use your painting as a PR ploy."

"No, no," said Mrs. Potts gruffly, waving Eula aside. "Pottses never cancel events. I trust Walt here to figure out what happened to *Heifer in Tomato Patch*."

We all looked askance at this statement, since Walt's a hard-working guy, but since there's only one of him and he's usually dealing with things like bar fights at the Bryn Mawr Pub and lost cats. However, Honey's faith in Walt was touching, and seemed to give him a confidence boost.

"Why was the painting here at the club, exactly, again?" Walt asked her gently. "And how many people knew it here?"

"*Heifer in Tomato Patch* is one of the only pieces of English pastoral art that features my two passions in life," explained Mrs. Potts. "The Potts family has always been devoted to both cattle and tomatoes."

"Uh-huh," said Walt, as everyone's eyes except Eula's glazed over, since she's an avid grower of Early Girls herself.

Predictably, Holly and the Colketts had zero interest in the subject of the party they were planning, since tomato growing was generally done by a more senior group of Bryn Mawr stalwarts.

In fact, so obsessed is the town by the tasty veggie that Saturday's event was part one of the Tomato Show, which includes the kickoff party and the Early Girl competition. Part two of the show happens a couple of weeks later, and features about forty-five additional categories of said plant that ripen at the end of July.

As Mrs. Potts explained that the painting was the centerpiece of her annual Tomato Show lecture, I saw Sophie and Bootsie exchange an eye roll and start checking their phones, with Sophie clicking on what looked like the Neiman Marcus Web site. To be honest, it did sound like the lecture could have been a bit of a snooze.

"And a lot of people knew the painting would be here?" continued Walt.

"This *Bryn Mawr Gazette* had it on the front page last Thursday," said Honey, indicating Bootsie with an outstretched glass of vodka. "Bootsie wrote the story, so who knows, maybe that brought out the criminal element."

"Sorry." Bootsie shrugged. Guilt isn't an emotion Bootsie really experiences, which is why she's great at unearthing gossip and has an actual talent for digging up clues—or at least digging through personal belongings, medicine cabinets, and trash cans.

"So, everyone in town and anyone who reads the *Gazette* knew about the painting." Walt nodded. He closed his notebook and looked around the room. "Bootsie, I need you to run a favor past your boss at the paper," he told her. "Give me a day or two to get this painting back before you run a story about it."

"The horse is out of the barn, Walt," observed Mrs. Potts, clearing her throat and gulping down a bit of Smirnoff. "What's the difference now? And who knows, maybe whoever stole *Heifer* will get scared and bring it back."

Walt was shaking his head. "Media coverage usually hurts more than it helps," he told her. "First you get the weirdos, folks who claim to know where the painting is, or who try to find it themselves," he explained. "Also, say the person who stole this thing had no idea it's worth over a hundred grand. We don't want that information out there."

I felt for Walt. He looked tired and slightly rumpled.

"'I'm going to have Jared here gather all the club employees so we can ask if anyone saw anything unusual today, since most of the staff has been here all day today," he said.

"I'm on it!" said Jared enthusiastically, glancing at Holly to see if she'd noticed his initiative. She hadn't.

"While you're here, Tim and Tom, you helped Mrs. Potts hang this piece of art, correct?" Walt asked the Colketts in his mild way.

I could tell the Colketts immediately plunged straight into panic when asked this question, so I politely looked away, picking up a pamphlet describing the Tomato Show events, which actually featured *Heifer in Tomato Patch* on its cover.

I was impressed, honestly. The painting captured a stunning English estate backed by majestic green hills with a lake in the distance. No wonder Hasley Huntingdon-Mews paintings cost a mint! It was clear, even to my inexperienced eye, that it was a special painting, especially if you love cows as much as Honey Potts does. The heifer featured was a long-lashed beauty who projected a Marilyn Monroe–esque, come-hither gaze even while chewing cud. Everything about the painting screamed, *Old and rare!* and I could see why the Colketts were nervous.

"Well, we helped her for about four minutes," admitted Tom. "And, in my opinion, Tim totally fucked up the hanging height! I'd have gone four millimeters higher," Tom added, pointing a critical (and slightly boozy) finger toward the large picture hanger where *Heifer* had been. "And I told him, with a painting that size, we should have gone with two fifty-pound, double nail brass hangers, not that cheapo fifteen-pound steel one you used."

"It's always easier to be the one shouting out suggestions rather than doing actual *work*," sang out Tim.

"Walt, yell if you need us. We've got to get back to the furniture placement in the tent," announced Tom, as they vanished out a side door.

I need a drink, I thought.

Walt, meanwhile, announced that he, Jared, and Ronnie the club manager would search the club in case the painting had been misplaced and was still on the grounds. All staff and Trendy Tent employees should, for the moment, stay put.

"I'll help," said a male voice from the doorway. My stomach did a flip, since I knew this voice belonged to a tanned guy with dark beard stubble, muscly forearms, and an annoying but undeniable sexiness.

It was Mike Woodford, Honey's nephew, who lives in a cottage on her vast property and, naturally, shares the Potts passion for cows. In fact, Mike takes care of Honey's herd, and is her closest relative and heir apparent to all things Sanderson, which is the name of his aunt's beautiful old home.

I snuck a quick look at Mike, trying not to make eye contact, since that usually results in problems for me. Too much eye contact usually leads to forgetting that I have an amazing boyfriend and picturing myself and Mike in a steamy make-out scenario.

Last spring, I shared several such sessions with Mike. Then, the same week, I met an amazing, dependable, handsome veterinarian named John Hall, who I've been dating for more than a year now. John is an excellent boyfriend, in addition to being in great shape from playing a ton of tennis.

Since Mike Woodford is the kind of guy who makes out with you in a barn, then never calls you for three months, I've sworn to steer clear of him. Unfortunately, my boyfriend's devotion to his veterinary practice had sent him to a bovine medicine clinic this month, and he'd been in West Virginia for the past two weeks.

I needed to leave, and stay as far away as possible from Mike. This is something of a daily task for me, since Sanderson, where Mike and Honey both live, is right across the street from me. But I sternly reminded myself that I was practically immune to his dreamy brown eyes, tanned arms, and fantastic Irish Spring soap smell, which lingered in the Camellia Room after he and Jared left to go hunt for *Heifer*.

"Anyway, I've got that painting insured," Mrs. Potts told Walt. "As long as I'm covered once I took it off Sanderson property. I probably shoulda checked that."

"I'm going to call George Fogle, my friend who works at Sotheby's!" Holly announced. "He knows everything about art. He also knows tons about art thieves! George will probably be able to solve this crime with, like, three text messages and an Instagram post."

"Okay," said Mrs. Potts. "But don't cancel the party on my account."

Just then, a tall man with a gleaming bald head appeared in the doorway, a wooden crate full of feathered dead ducks in his muscly arms.

He wore a tight white T-shirt, skinny black leather pants, and gold earrings. His biceps were bedecked with depictions of the Leaning Tower of Pisa, the Roman Forum, and additional tattooed landmarks of his native land.

"The party is guaranteed to be amazing!" shouted the new arrival in a heavily accented voice. "Because I, Chef Gianni Brunello, star of my own Food Network show, am gonna cater your Tomato Party!"

Chapter 3

CHEF GIANNI WAS followed by small group of white-clad cooks and staff members, who he directed toward the club's kitchen. Walt, sensing he'd lost control of the situation, took off with Jared and Ronnie to do another search for *Heifer* in the rambling building, while Gianni held court, giving effusive greetings and hand kisses to Holly and Sophie.

He'd flown in to surprise Holly, he explained, since he'd suddenly found himself with a week off from his new restaurant venture and Food Network gig.

"Gianni, this is the club's chef, Skipper Parnell," Holly said politely as she introduced the two men. Skipper, a compact, one-time high school soccer star, is friendly with Bootsie's brothers from years of prep school competitions. Skipper went to culinary school ten years back, and after working in several high-end Philly restaurants, joined the club's staff the previous year. He'd quickly become a favorite for his deft hand with things like just the right amount of tarragon in the chicken salad, and fun theme nights featuring fondue and burger bars.

Skipper, who's pretty cute if you're into sporty, muscly guys who can cook, gave Gianni a friendly hello and handshake.

"Skipper, this is so last minute and I hope you won't hate me, but I'd forgotten that Gianni offered to do the food for the Tomato Show. That was months ago, before he got his own TV series!" Holly explained.

I remembered Holly telling me that Gianni had sat down at dinner with her and Howard one night at his Bryn Mawr restaurant before he began his California Food Network gig, and that the chef had bragged that he'd show the country club crowd what real Italian food was at her party. Naturally, she'd figured this was bullshit and that Gianni would never show up—but here he was, ready to cook.

Actually, the timing seemed a little strange.

"I not gonna let you down, Holly Jones, you gorgeous girl!" Gianni told her. "Although, to be honest, I'm too famous to be doing this party, but Gianni gets bored if he's not busy!"

"So, and this will obviously be the newest trend in party planning, we can have you *both* catering the event," Holly told Skipper and Gianni.

"Hey, man, welcome," Skipper said politely to Gianni. "Of course, we'd love to have you help out Saturday night in the kitchen."

"Gianni is celebrity chef with tons of awards," said the Italian chef. "Gianni don't 'help.'"

Skipper's too polite to complain, but he looked upset as he disappeared through the kitchen's swinging double doors. It had to be a bitter blow to have been working on the party menu for weeks and have Gianni show up and steal his thunder.

"Obviously, it's fabulous that you'll be cooking Saturday,"

Holly told Gianni. "But aren't you supposed to be opening your restaurant in California in, like, four days?"

"It's gonna be delayed a couple weeks," Gianni said, waving dismissively. "'Cause my camera guys and busboys been complaining they need a day off every three weeks! Those guys all whiners! And someone tip off Department of Labor out in California, so I get some *stupida* warning letter about employees working too many hours."

"Uh-huh," said Holly, nodding, while Bootsie and I exchanged an eye roll. Gianni was widely known as the world's worst boss. "Well, anyway, poor Mrs. Potts has had a really hard day. She had her favorite painting stolen."

"She lose a painting—big deal!" opined the chef. "Gianni fly in from California, then I find out some report a suitcase of pancetta and soppressata I checked, and it got seized by the FDA!" Gianni told us, handing off his crate of birds to a passing Trendy Tent employee, who wisely didn't argue that it wasn't his job, and headed toward the kitchen.

We all sighed. Gianni's in negative range on the empathy meter—not that Mrs. Potts cared. I noticed her shrugging and preparing to leave via a side entrance. She doesn't deal with the Giannis of this world. "I'll drive you, Aunt Honey," said Mike Woodford, who'd returned with Jared. He offered the doyenne his arm and they disappeared—but not before I caught a glimpse of his long-lashed brown eyes.

"I had to have big fight with guys at baggage claim over my secret stash of meat!" complained Gianni. "Someone call to complain that it's not sanitary to bring uncured pork products on a flight. Big deal. Everyone jealous of Gianni, and trying to screw him over!"

This was interesting, I thought. The Colketts came to mind as possible tattletales about Gianni's skirting California labor laws, though they were said to be earning a hefty fee from Gianni for their design work, plus they were getting paid to be on his Food Network show. And any one of his staff might have made the calls to the FDA, since probably every one of them had some beef with the chef.

"Uh, boss?" Skipper came back from the kitchen, his polo shirt damp around the collar with perspiration and his handsome face registering anger. "Listen, Ronnie, I can't work like this. This guy"—here, he indicated Gianni—"told my staff to pack up our equipment and take it out to the golf shed. He's bringing in his own pans and has his staff moving all our meats and vegetables to the back of the walk-in fridge to make room for his ducks."

Ronnie, the club manager, normally the most unflappable and low-key of men, manages with a seemingly effortless style that keeps everything from the chicken salad to the golf greens in perfect working order. The only time I've ever seen him frazzled was when my elderly neighbor Jimmy Best moved into the club for a few days last spring, and drove the staff crazy with constant demands for Scotch and fresh towels.

Today, though, Ronnie showed a slight sheen of perspiration around his temples, his hair was slightly ruffled, and there was a wrinkle in his Lands' End khakis.

"Try to ignore him," Ronnie said, sotto voce. "I'll deal with him tomorrow."

"I am so sorry, Skipper," Holly told him. "Also, are we suspects, Walt?" she added. "Because I wouldn't mind being considered a possible criminal mastermind, but if not, I need to get out of here and away from Eula Morris."

"I doubt you'd steal a painting from a party you've been planning for months," said Walt with a faint smile. "Bootsie already told me she was driving back from Maine and just got back in town an hour ago, so she couldn't have stolen the thing."

Just then, the Colketts tiptoed past the slightly open door to the Camellia Room—almost making an escape, but not quite.

"Hey, Colketts! You guys supposed to be in California!" Gianni screamed. "Working on my new place! I give the painters and construction guys the week off, but I never tell you to take vacation."

"When the painters and stonemasons for the pizza oven said they weren't coming in this week, Chef, we figured we could take a little time off, too," Tim told him, looking terrified as he took a tentative step inside the space—which I was personally desperate to flee. "I mean, we worked forty-two days straight."

"Everyone lazy except Gianni!" said the chef. "But anyway, that's okay, I can respect you guys do a little sneaking around. Gianni forgive you for lying to him! But now that I know you're here, I gonna get you guys to help me build a fire pit over by tennis court, with a customized smoker I gonna put the ducks in for eighteen hours before I make my ragout for Saturday night."

"The club has a gas grill that you're welcome to use," Ronnie informed him.

"I don't use gas grill," said Gianni. "Which is why Colketts gonna make me a smoker."

"Um, Chef, we don't really do things like build fire pits," Tom said nervously. "Or customize smokers."

"If Gianni say you make me a smoker, you going to," said the chef, his face turning purple as he stalked out of the Camellia Room. "And you know what, you guys gonna help me pluck my ducks first! Meet me in the kitchen in two minutes!"

Luckily for the Colketts, at that moment, Gianni got distracted by a passing waitress.

I'd noticed this adorable girl the last few times I'd been at the club—she was a sweet-natured college student on summer break, named Abby, and possessed the upbeat personality and long blond curls that sent men's necks swiveling in her direction.

Also, Abby has fabulous boobs. She even makes the club's uniform—a dark green, boxy polo shirt—look sexy, which isn't all that easy to do.

"Hey, blondie," shouted Gianni. "You real cute! Maybe you come work for Gianni!" At this, Abby gave a started look over her shoulder, and bolted toward the kitchen doors.

"Don't ya have a girlfriend-hyphen-assistant right now, Gianni?" asked Sophie. "I know you're a real ladies' man!"

This is actually true. When Gianni wants to, he turns on the charm and is actually irresistible to women from ages eighteen to eighty.

There's something undeniably sexy about him when he's in his element welcoming guests to his restaurants, presenting some delicious dish, or even when he's doing unbelievably over-the-top kissing and inappropriate squeezing of women of a certain age whose husbands don't mind spending two hundred and fifty dollars on dinner.

"I been too busy," Gianni told Sophie, "but I gotta find new girlfriend soon. Gianni needs the sex! How about you, Sophie? You still dating that guy who picks out your sofas?"

"Absolutely," said Sophie proudly. "My Honey Bunny and I are totally in love!"

"That's too bad. But I date you if you dump him!" Gianni told her, giving Sophie a bunch of hand kisses and a lascivious grope.

"Anyway, Gianni got to make a quick phone call." With that, he disappeared.

A neatly dressed guy popped his head into the room—a new member of club management, I guessed, since he had an official air.

"Is there a Mrs. Sophie Shields here?" he asked politely. "I have a delivery."

"That's me!" said Sophie, waving at him excitedly. "Do ya have flowers for me? Maybe it's a box of long-stemmed roses from Joe!"

"Not exactly," said the guy, reaching into his pockets and pulling out an envelope, which he handed to a startled Sophie. "This is notice from your estranged husband's legal representatives. You need to vacate your new home on Begonia Lane, list it for sale immediately, and escrow half the proceeds to be given to Mr. Shields.

"Also," said the preppy guy, looking distinctly uncomfortable, "your ex is demanding that you turn over joint property in the form of twenty-two pairs of Gucci sandals, size five and a half, which he says he bought you on your honeymoon in Venice, Italy. He says you'll know why he wants them. Um—have a nice night!" he added, turning on his loafered heel and disappearing.

For once, Sophie was speechless. Her tiny hand went to her heart—currently clad in a silk Lilly P. minidress—and she looked down at her shoes, which were gold four-inch-high numbers, and appeared to be one of the twenty-two pairs of Guccis under subpoena.

Just then, a crash of glass and heavy furniture erupted in the bar.

"*Merda!*" came a scream.

Chapter 4

WALT AND JARED arrived in the barroom at the same time we did, where Gianni was flat on the ground in front of the darkened mahogany bar, a bottle of Macallan smashed next to him alongside a heavy rocks glass. Gianni was facedown, the back of his be-earringed bald head looking oddly vulnerable as he lay there moaning. A steely, sharp knife was stuck through his leather pants into the back of his thigh.

"Ohmigosh!" screamed Sophie. "Chef, did ya fall on a knife and stab yourself?"

"How I gonna fall facedown and stab myself in the back of my leg?" Gianni yelled at her, pointing at the blade. "Gianni was attacked from behind by some kind of crazed killer—probably that sore loser, Skipper!"

"Should we, you know, wiggle the knife out?" asked Bootsie, as Officer Walt turned on the lights and dialed 911 for an ambulance. "Because it looks kind of painful."

"Those rugs just came in from Savafieh, so I wouldn't yank on that blade," Holly said, shrugging. "Howard and I just paid to redecorate this room, since I think the old carpets in here were from 1902. Although, given this incident, we probably should have waited."

She bent over to give a sympathetic assessment of Gianni—who didn't seem to be oozing all that much blood. His tight leather pants were seemingly acting as a giant tourniquet. "Can I get you anything, Chef? Maybe a nice martini?"

"I'm bleeding to death here!" screamed Gianni, who tried to turn over but then moaned even louder.

"Even more reason to break out the Grey Goose," Holly told him.

"I took a CPR course in college, and I'm pretty sure leg wounds are rarely fatal," Bootsie announced.

"Fuck you!" responded Gianni.

"Jared, please go outside and direct the EMTs when they get here," Walt said calmly. "Now, Chef Gianni, what happened?"

"How the hell I know?" shouted the chef. "I come into bar to grab myself a drink. I see the Scotch sitting right at end of counter, so I reach over to pour myself a big one when suddenly Gianni feels the worst pain of his life!

"I fall facedown and so I never get good look at this person, but I get quick glance over my shoulder and I see it was some short guy wearing green polo shirt, like everyone wear at this *putana* country club. So Gianni is one hundred percent sure it was Skipper!" Just then, Skipper himself poked his head into the bar, his face frozen with apparently genuine shock as he took in the scene before him.

"I was back in the kitchen this whole time!" Skipper protested. "I didn't do this to you."

Gianni turned his head to glare at him, which wasn't all that effective given his prone position. "Skipper, you nothing but a glorified burger flipper. You try to murder me out of insane jealousy, but you never gonna keep Gianni down!"

TWENTY MINUTES LATER, Gianni had been rolled out on a gurney (still facedown, since the medics explained that it's really not a good idea to remove a freshly plunged-in knife). The instrument used appeared to be Gianni's own deboning blade—which he'd left out in the kitchen, ready to tackle his ducks.

At seven-fifteen, as dusk was falling outside, Officer Walt told us we were free to go. I needed to go to bed early and be up early for a full day of painting my shop.

Additionally, I'm currently dog-sitting four motley mutts belonging to my boyfriend of one year, John Hall. And Waffles, my adored hound, likes to eat at 6 p.m sharp, so he was going to be miffed. I started explaining all this, but Sophie turned sad brown eyes on me, tears welling up, and told me she needed all her friends around her after her the process server incident.

"I need pasta," Sophie wailed. "I eat when I'm stressed."

"This is the perfect night to go to Gianni's restaurant for dinner, since he'll be stuck in the ER for hours," Holly said, turning on her elegant Prada heel. "We can discuss Sophie's divorce problems and solve the mystery of who stabbed Gianni."

"Okay," I relented. "I've got to go get Waffles and then feed the herd of dogs at my house. See you there in twenty minutes."

RISTORANTE GIANNI, IN the charming old Bryn Mawr Firehouse, was in lively full swing tonight, even on a Thursday. It's a stylish bistro the temperamental chef opened last year before fame had beckoned him to California, and is the most sought-after reservation in town. The old stone firehouse was always an appealing building, but after its restaurant redo, the place is absolutely gorgeous, with French doors that are thrown open on warm nights, a long glossy bar, and an antique wooden chandelier brought back from Italy.

There's a pretty stone patio and lots of potted trees and plants, votive candles everywhere, and the whole place is scented with heavenly rosemary, tomatoes bubbling on the stove, grilling meats, and other fragrances designed to compel the moneyed crowd who dines here into splurging on things like forty-two-dollar veal chops and five-hundred-dollar bottles of wine.

And believe me, it works. Gianni brags that he earns suitcases full of cash every night here—which kind of makes you wonder about how much he's declaring in taxes.

Anyway, I'd stopped back at The Striped Awning, picked up Waffles, and taken him home to my tiny cottage, which happens to be right across the street from Sanderson.

All four of John's dogs were on my living room couch, wagging and drooling, when I got in, and I sighed as they burst out into the backyard with Waffles. I dished up five servings of kibbles, refilled the water bowls, and gave everyone some petting and belly rubs. I threw on a new coat of lip gloss, grabbed my keys, and locked the back door as the dogs headed back for the couch, fur flying everywhere.

Now, it was 8 p.m., which is around the time I like to jump into bed. I'd stay for one glass of wine and head home pronto.

"Your usual table, Ms. Jones?" asked a teenage hostess in a black Gap dress—which I realized with some devastation that I had in my own closet. I'm not sure an antiques dealer in her thirties, even one who's as broke as I am, should have the same dress as a girl who looked like she was about seventeen years old.

"Did you hear about what happened to our boss, by the way?" she added. "He got stabbed! In the leg, which sounds really painful!"

Behind her, the bartenders grinned happily, and some of the busboys gave a happy fist pump.

"Absolutely," said Holly airily. "We were in the next room when it happened, but unfortunately we missed the actual attack. Anyway, my favorite table is the one over near the French doors, but anywhere Gianni can't see us in the unlikely event he gets sprung quickly from the hospital is perfect."

The hostess giggled and led us through the already crowded dining area to a white-clothed table to the right of the bar area. I liked this table, too, because between the dogs and my paint job, I honestly looked pretty terrible. I sighed—Ristorante Gianni isn't the kind of place where you want to show up ponytailed and with pink paint in your hair.

The two times I've eaten here, I've seen about forty-five people I know, including Bootsie's parents, Eula Morris, Mike Woodford, and even Leena, the woman who runs the Pack-N-Ship.

"Isn't this kinda boring back here?" Sophie pouted. "I like it up front, right where you can see when everyone walks in!" I knew Bootsie would agree with Sophie, but luckily she'd actually decided to stop home, see her children and Will, and offload her L.L. Bean haul, and wasn't here yet.

I'd resolved to stay for one drink, since I currently had eleven dollars in crumpled ones in my wallet. I really don't want Holly and Sophie pay my bar tabs and meals anymore. It was one thing when we were in Florida and my two moneybags friends owned the restaurant we ate in most nights, but I'd vowed to myself this summer that I'd pay my own way.

Maybe I could hit the bread basket and then get Sophie to take me home, I thought, as a waiter passed by bearing what looked like a lobster spaghetti dish that looked absolutely delicious.

"Who picked this table?" said Bootsie, popping up behind me, and to be honest, scaring me as she suddenly leaned over the table to grab the handwritten list of specials.

"I'll have a glass of the California pinot noir!" I said to the waiter after I'd checked which was the least expensive vintage sold by the glass. He nodded politely, but his expression read that I was the first customer ever at Ristorante Gianni who'd shown up with a handful of bills dug out from the bottom of an Old Navy tote bag.

"Cancel that and bring us two bottles of the Sangiovese," Holly told him.

Meanwhile, Sophie was furiously texting her lawyers about the legal papers she'd been served at the club, and venting.

"Just when Joe and I finally have my closet fully customized—and by the way, it's awesome, with special handbag shelving and cubbies designed for boots, booties, wedges, and stilettos—*now* Barclay decides it's joint property?" shrieked Sophie. "He already has our old house. Plus Barclay hates antiques and is afraid of houses built before 1980! I guarantee he'd have an aneurysm if he had to ever set foot in my place, which was built in 1932!"

I nodded sympathetically, taking in the scene around me. I was starving, and couldn't stop thinking about that lobster dish that had just sailed by.

At least I'm not eating Progresso soup *every* night anymore, I thought hopefully, since I've been dating John. He's not a great cook, either, but he does have a grill, and we sometimes end up barbecuing a steak or some chicken.

I'm embarrassed to have Holly pay for yet another meal for me, but she reminded me that her husband is one of the silent partners in Gianni's restaurant, and that it was incumbent upon us to eat and drink heartily here, since Gianni pays back his investors in pasta.

"We *have* to eat here," Holly informed me.

"Mr. Jones is awesome!" said the waiter, suddenly coming to life. "Sorry, I'm new here, but I've heard all about your husband. He's the best investor we ever had here at Gianni! He's got an unlimited tab, and he authorized an automatic thirty percent tip on top of any meal.

"Let me bring you something to snack on. I'm thinking these really teeny-tiny lamb chops we do with rosemary, and the risotto Milanese. Be right back with those and the wine!"

Chapter 5

"So far, your Tomato Party is a disaster," Bootsie told Holly as she dug into the first appetizers seven minutes later. "You've had a painting stolen, Chef Gianni got stabbed, and you've spent most of the past few months arguing with Eula Morris."

"Having a painting stolen is totally fabulous!" Holly told her. "That plus a stabbing *makes* the party. I mean, I feel badly for Mrs. Potts and everything," she added, "but trust me, Gianni will be up and cooking Saturday, and the tent will be packed!" She nibbled half an olive thoughtfully. "You have a point about Eula, though."

"Luckily for you, I've already solved the painting problem," Bootsie informed her. "I'm pretty sure Gianni took it. Before he got stabbed, obviously," she added.

"Didn't Gianni say he flew in this afternoon and got stuck at the airport trying to free his unregulated pork?" I asked Bootsie. "How could he have stolen the painting if he wasn't even in town yet?"

"Gianni's lying," she said confidently. "I'm going to make sure Walt checks with the airline and the customs people. Gianni probably flew back here a couple days ago, and made the whole thing up about the prosciutto problem."

"I love prosciutto!" said Sophie, nibbling risotto. "It reminds me of Joe, too, even though he told me pork makes him bloated. And then he doesn't want to get any lovin' because he feels fat!"

"Thanks for sharing that, Sophie," said Joe, who'd just appeared at the table.

"Honey Bunny!" shrieked Sophie, throwing herself into his arms. "You're back from Florida just in time for two new crimes!"

WANTING TO SURPRISE Sophie by returning a day early, Joe had texted Holly and learned we were at Gianni's. He'd come right from the airport, but somehow managed to look unrumpled in khakis, sock-free loafers, and a polo, and listened to a quick download of the day's events as he simultaneously downed a glass of red wine.

"I guess it's possible someone else at the club could have gone into the Camellia Room and grabbed *Heifer in Tomato Patch*," Bootsie said, forking in some agnolotti with morel mushrooms. I'd gotten one bite of this incredible dish before it landed in front of Bootsie, at which point it seemed to have reached its final destination.

We hadn't actually ordered anything, because once the waiter had made the Howard-Holly connection, he'd started bringing dish after dish. Things like Barolo-marinated short ribs and polenta with pecorino were now deliciously crowding the table.

"Wouldn't someone notice a painting being walked down the main hallway of the club past the bar and the dining room?" asked Joe. "Didn't you say the thing has a big gilt frame?"

"It was complete chaos, thanks to Eula," Holly told him. "The

Colketts and I were completely organized and were working with a small group of trusted staff from The Trendy Tent there, but Eula was a disaster. Every time the Colketts had the chandeliers in the perfect spot, she'd ask them some dumb question about fire safety, or demand that we make more space to showcase the tomatoes—like anyone except her and Bootsie's mom cares about those dumb plants."

"How did you end up in charge of this party again?" Joe asked. "You don't garden, and you hate Eula."

"I care about tradition," Holly said airily. "I wanted to support an important event honoring heirloom garden techniques."

"I thought you wanted to stick it to Eula," Bootsie said, digging into a grilled langoustine.

"That, too. By the way, Eula could have taken the painting," Holly said. "And in fact, I think she did!"

We all paused to think this over for a moment.

"Also, Eula could have easily stabbed Gianni," said Holly.

Eula as art thief and knife-wielding attempted murderess? I could see her stealing a cake recipe off the Internet and passing it off as her own, but taking Honey's painting and then managing to shop it around on the international art market just didn't seem like Eula.

"Eula's short and stubby, but she's a good golfer and tennis player," mused Joe. "I guess she could schlep a heavy painting out to her Miata—if it fit in the trunk. And she's got a lot of upper body strength, so stabbing someone would be no big deal."

"Gianni said a guy in a polo shirt tried to debone him," I told him, shaking my head. "Eula had on her usual outfit today—beige dress, beige pumps."

"Everyone knows the staff uniforms are in the break room

inside the kitchen," Joe told me. "It would take Eula two seconds to go in there, borrow a polo shirt and shorts, and stab Gianni. And despite her size, she's very manly."

Interestingly, Joe's one of the few people I know who isn't afraid of Eula. Since Eula's quite vindictive, most people won't stand up to her, but Joe lobs insults at her whenever he gets the chance.

"I guess it's possible," I said. "It's true that Eula was nowhere to be seen after Gianni got nailed in the leg."

"You know what—I'm going to over to Eula's tonight!" shouted Bootsie, attracting annoyed glances from neighboring tables. "And I'm going to watch that crazy bitch through her living room windows till I catch her with either Honey's painting or a blood-stained polo shirt!"

WITH THIS, BOOTSIE downed some more wine and texted her husband, Will, that she had some *Gazette* reporting to do and would be home late.

"You know, the Colketts could have grabbed Honey's painting, and I peg them as the stabbers—one of them could have been on look-out while the other did the deed with the duck knife," Bootsie told us.

Honestly, I thought, Bootsie always throws the Colketts into the ring as suspects of every crime in our town. So far they've never been the culprits, but they *are* actually on the spot most of the time whenever anything nefarious goes down. It seems that they're merely often at the wrong place at the wrong time.

"The Colketts are nice guys, but they have expensive taste, and who knows, maybe they have an obsession with antique paint-ings!" Bootsie continued. "And if they attacked Gianni, they'd probably get an award and a party thrown for them by anyone who's ever worked for the guy."

"Amen to that," said the waiter, dropping off another bottle of wine.

"How was the kitchen organizing, Honey Bunny?" Sophie asked Joe, still clinging to him with both arms. "Did ya get the Bernardaud plates in the cabinet the way you and Mrs. Earle wanted?"

"It was a *huge* battle that took a lot of margaritas to get Mrs. E. to agree to my plate placement," Joe complained. Mrs. Earle, a sweet-tempered but boozy tobacco heiress, has a beautiful old Florida home that Joe was helping to update. Luckily, he had the assistance of her butler, who had tired of a kitchen dating back to 1967.

Joe whipped out his iPad from his ever-present tote bag, and showed us pictures of his kitchen update. The look was indeed fantastic, with glossy white cabinets, gorgeous crystal hardware, and a fabulous chandelier over a modern table.

"Uh-huh," said Sophie. "So, are ya done down in Florida?"

"There's a possibility I'll need to go back down and work on an installation of forks and napkins next week," said Joe.

Holly and I rolled our eyes at this. Even Holly doesn't hire Joe for tasks this minor.

"Anyway, I have some info, too," Joe told us, not looking too happy. "Someone we all know and don't love was on my flight up from West Palm Beach. Let me give you a hint: She was wearing a tracksuit."

Just then, over the jaunty Ella Fitzgerald tunes being piped through the sound system and the buzz of happy diners, another familiar voice made its way through the old firehouse and made landfall at our table.

"I don't care what Mr. Shields said on phone! Cancel the pappardelle. Barclay, he only supposed to eat steamed fish and veggies." All heads swiveled to regard a tall, muscular woman in a black Nike outfit at the bar, opening a huge bag of take-out food and removing plastic containers of delicious pastas and risottos.

There was some polite arguing from the bartender, who was trying to hand over four additional bags of takeout.

"Barclay, who pays me to keep him healthy, is gonna die from the cholesterol if you give him this food! Meat and pasta, all poison!" said the woman, whose back was to us.

Joe froze, half a grilled langoustine on his fork and midway to his mouth.

"That's who was sitting behind me on the plane," he moaned.

Only one person we knew would make a stand against pasta in the middle of Bryn Mawr's best Italian restaurant.

Gerda.

It was Sophie's former live-in Pilates pro, and Joe's worst nightmare.

Chapter 6

"GERDA!" SHRIEKED SOPHIE happily. She jumped up and ran to the bar, where she reached up on her tiny stilettoed tiptoes to hug her friend and erstwhile personal trainer.

"Come over to our table!" she urged Gerda, who shrugged and followed Sophie to where we all sat, trailed by a sous-chef and the bartender, who was nervously toting the unwanted dishes.

"Listen, lady, we don't like to upset Mr. Shields," he told Gerda nervously. "Chef Gianni told us when we opened this place last summer that whatever Barclay Shields wants is an automatic yes. I guess they're old friends. Plus the chef seems a little afraid of Mr. Shields," he added, sotto voce.

"Lot of people scared of Barclay." Gerda nodded, handing back containers of ravioli and tagliatelle. "Luckily, I'm not one of them." The guy looked uncertain, but reluctantly disappeared through the crowd with the rejected pastas.

"Hi, Gerda," said Holly with a little wave.

Gerda is one of the more unlikely residents of our town: An Austrian-born fitness expert, she'd met Sophie and Barclay several years back when the Shieldses were honeymooning in Venice. Distracted by the sight of a Versace boutique, Sophie had almost slipped into a canal, and Gerda had saved her from a foot-first plunge into the murky depths. They'd exchanged e-mail addresses and thanked Gerda profusely, then continued on their tour of Italy.

But to the Shieldses' surprise, Gerda had showed up unannounced in Bryn Mawr and moved into their guest room, where she'd remained for two years. After Sophie split from Barclay, a fortuitous health crisis had forced Barclay—a lover of all things meat—to hire Gerda as live-in trainer and nutritionist, since doctors had ordered him to lose thirty percent of his body weight.

Gerda's new job had paved the way for Sophie and Joe to have an actual romance, since there was no way Joe could amorously interact with his girlfriend with Gerda in the same house. Joe's greatest fear, though, was the return of Gerda—if Barclay ever got svelte enough to ditch her. Luckily, so far, Barclay had apparently kept her on as his personal food police, and none of us had seen her since January—until now.

Holly and Gerda had struck up an improbable alliance over the winter in Florida, where we'd gotten caught up in a swirl of events including trying to save a historic old schoolhouse that was almost torn down for condos. The erstwhile developer, one Scooter Simmons, had developed a crush on Holly, who'd met him for drinks one night to, well, pump him for information, and Gerda had served as her bodyguard, in case Scooter got too hands-y with Holly.

"I didn't know ya were coming back to Bryn Mawr!" Sophie said happily. "Come have a drink with us. Or a club soda, if you're still anti-booze."

"Okay," said Gerda. What I think was a smile appeared on her tanned and makeup-free face. "Got to be real quick, though. Barclay waiting for food, and he get really pissy when he don't get it fast enough.

"I notice though that Barclay in an excellent mood," Gerda added. "He decide to fly back up from Miami yesterday, and he real happy. You know what that means."

"It means he's about to screw someone over in a business deal, and make a ton of money!" yelled Sophie.

"Uh-huh. That's what I think, too." Gerda nodded. "And I think one of those people he about to double-cross is you, Sophie."

SOPHIE FUMED FOR a few minutes while Gerda explained that Barclay had been locked in the office of the fortieth-floor Miami condo he'd rented since January, whispering about a mysterious deal at all hours of the day and night. Luckily, he'd been eating at a pricey steakhouse called The Forge a few times a week, so Gerda had been able to regularly hack into and browse through his e-mail correspondence at will.

"I think Barclay suspected I was looking at his e-mail, so he was being careful what he write," Gerda said. "What I can see is he got money in a few deals in Florida, and one new condo deal over in Vegas. But there's one thing I see a few e-mails about that's up here in Pennsylvania—something about a farm. I don't get it, 'cause Barclay don't like to go outside, so there's no way he gonna grow, like, squash and broccoli.

"Anyway, a coupla weeks ago, he put new password on his computer, so I don't know the latest," Gerda finished.

Vowing that she'd get half of whatever new venture her soon-to-be-ex was cooking up, Sophie jumped up and disappeared on her teetery sandals into to the ladies' room to call her lawyer.

"Did you finally get your driver's license?" Bootsie asked, with her usual lack of tact, while Joe got up and politely pulled over a chair from a neighboring table for Gerda. Joe has excellent manners, even though he'd rather be anywhere else than at dinner with Gerda. I also noticed him gulping down a Xanax that Holly had handed over immediately upon Gerda's arrival.

"I fail driving test down in Miami," Gerda said grimly. "Barclay was supposed to give me driving lessons, but he too busy with work. Then he had dental surgery and took so many painkillers he couldn't do nothing. I still got no license, but I got Uber waiting outside."

"Barclay always did have impacted teeth!" said Sophie with evident satisfaction as she returned to the table. "My lawyer didn't pick up," she added, "but I'm going to his office first thing tomorrow. Barclay isn't going to get away with cheating me out of one more dime in this divorce."

"I help you, Sophie," said Gerda, a small smile creasing her dry lips. "Barclay a real jerk lately, so I'm in the mood to make problems for him. I can go through his e-mail once I figure out his new password.

"Plus that dentist nailed Barclay pretty good. His face swollen for two weeks, and he lose fifteen pounds. Anyway, tomorrow Barclay leaves for a week in Atlantic City for some secret business meetings, so I got plenty of free time coming up.

"Who knows, maybe he don't need me anymore," announced Gerda. "I could quit my job and move back in with you, Sophie!"

THINGS SPIRALED FOR Joe after Gerda made this announcement.

Sophie made some noncommittal but positive noises about Gerda staying with her "for a few days, that would be fun!" while giving Joe nervous glances.

"Gerda, I don't think you should leave your job with Barclay," Holly told the Pilates pro. "But since he's going out of town, I'm going to hire you for the next few days to help me with a party at the country club. You have the perfect personality to deal with Chef Gianni and the Colketts."

"Sure, I help you out," agreed Gerda. "I meet you there tomorrow morning at 8 a.m. sharp."

"Make it ten-thirty," Holly told her.

Joe, meanwhile, waved down the waiter for a double vodka, and Bootsie surprised me by getting up to leave when I did.

"Hey, aren't you Gianni's camera guy?" Bootsie said to a cute twenty-something guy in a navy T-shirt and jeans who was doing a shot at the bar as we passed it on our way out.

"Yup," said the guy boozily. "I'm Randy. Gianni insisted I film him going to the ER, which he says will make great TV. I was over at the hospital until half an hour ago. Gianni's gonna be fine, by the way. The deboning knife is really thin, and it landed in a muscle, so it's just a matter of sewing him up. Anyway, Gianni booked me into the Peach Creek Motel out on the highway, which is a total dive. I'd rather sit here and drink."

As we left, a tiny elderly lady in a black skirt, black blouse, and white apron bid the chatty hostess a rather stern "*Buona notte*," and headed out the door and to a flight of stairs that presumably led to her apartment, which had been the kitchen and lounge when this building had served as the Bryn Mawr Firehouse.

"So there really is a pasta lady who lives upstairs?" Bootsie asked the hostess.

"There sure is!" the Gap-clad teen assured her. "She and her cat Bianca are up there, which is kinda creepy. But then I also feel kinda bad for her! She has to deal with Gianni a lot. He even flew her out to Beverly Hills to work at his new place, but she hated it and demanded to come back here. Supposedly she made it into the Food Network show for a few episodes, though, and she gets her name into the title credits."

As I crossed the parking lot and got into my slightly dented Subaru, I saw the light from a TV flicker on upstairs in the apartment of the charming old building. Was Nonna Claudia lonely, I wondered, or was Bianca enough companionship after a full day of pasta making? Maybe she was one of those single-minded people for whom work was everything. A perfect, pillowy gnocchi or pappardelle might be enough for Nonna Claudia. I sighed. Waffles and I weren't all that different from Claudia and her cat, when I thought about it, although we were still in the same town where we'd always lived, which afforded a certain comfort. How, exactly, had Chef Gianni gotten this lady to leave her home and share her genius for pasta with greater Philly, and did she regret having packed up her rolling pin and pasta machine for leafy Bryn Mawr?

For a moment, I wondered if Claudia might have been the tipster who'd ratted out Gianni to the FDA, but then dismissed the idea. She was probably just what she seemed: a lady whose passion for pasta ruled her existence.

Chapter 7

THE NEXT MORNING, a slight hangover mingled with paint fumes combined to give me a headache that didn't improve with the arrival of Eula Morris, who stopped by at 10 a.m. with three framed still-lifes of tomatoes that she'd personally painted.

"The Colketts told me these don't work with their vision for the party," she told me sourly. "Which is ridiculous. I mean, how do tomatoes I depicted in the style of Cezanne *not* convey tomatoes? Anyway, I thought maybe you could sell them here at The Striped Awning."

The paintings were cute enough, I thought: two larger canvases, and another tiny one about eight inches square, all in antique gilt frames. I told Eula she could leave them on consignment, and she zoomed away in her Miata. Next up was Bootsie, who came at one-thirty with a delivery of a late lunch.

"Nothing happened at Eula's last night," she said, handing me chicken salad on toasted white from the luncheonette. "I sat in a tree in her backyard and watched her for forty-five minutes through her living room window. She misted her tomato plants, put on her pajamas, and watched HGTV for forty-five minutes. She has a bunch of paintings hanging in her house, but *Heifer in Tomato Patch* wasn't one of them. And she was in her beige dress, not a blood-spattered polo shirt."

"That's so creepy of you," I told Bootsie as I munched half my sandwich and gave the rest to Waffles, who thumped his tail happily as he ate. Bootsie shook her head disapprovingly—her yellow Labs eat organic kibbles and never enjoy the fatty snacks that Waffles gets, which is why Bootsie's dogs are slim and fit, and Waffles is, well, portly in a dignified and adorable way.

"I mean, you sitting out there in the dark, watching her. That's super-weird!"

"What—you don't do that?" Bootsie asked. "Anyway, I'm a reporter! And Walt doesn't have the manpower to do surveillance. I'm helping the community."

She shrugged. "And, anyway, Eula went into her bedroom to change into her PJs, and she pulled her blinds down. What's the big deal?"

I sighed.

"Anyway, here's our story on Gianni getting stabbed, which will have to hold over the public till Walt lifts the news embargo on the stolen painting," she added, handing over the *Gazette*. "Obviously, my photos and Gianni story are page one. I texted it into my editor while I was sitting outside on Eula's patio," she added.

I scanned Bootsie's story—really, more of a paragraph, since Walt had said he couldn't comment on an open investigation and had no official suspects.

Luckily, Bootsie's editor is accustomed to her random and unsubstantiated theories, and always edits out her personal opinions, so the story about Gianni merely noted that buzz around town suggested that there were plenty of people with a grudge against the chef, including employees who complained that the chef forced them to work tons of hours and never honored requests for time off.

"It's hard to find anyone who *wouldn't* want to stab the chef, actually," mused Bootsie, wadding up her sandwich wrapping and making a neat three-point shot into my trash can. "It's not just the Colketts who hate him. I mean, he forced one waiter to cancel his honeymoon last year, and when his sous-chef's wife had twins in April, he had to be back at work the next morning! Plus he has that elderly pasta lady working every single night, although I doubt she stabbed him. Anyway, all his staff admits that Gianni pays well and their tips are great. They make too much money to quit."-

I pondered this as I poured paint into a plastic tray. I could only imagine the tips left on the hefty checks that diners were handed at the conclusion of a meal at Gianni's.

"I'd love to moonlight at Gianni's myself and make some extra cash," I admitted to Bootsie. "But I can't cook, I'd never be able to memorize all the specials, and I'm not good at balancing trays."

"You don't have the cleavage for it," Bootsie told me, looking skeptically at my T-shirt. "Even if you got one of those Bombshell Bras at Victoria's Secret, Gianni would never hire you. Speaking of jobs, though, I saw Leena from the Pack-N-Ship over at the luncheonette, and she said you could take on a weekend shift," Bootsie told me. "I told her how broke you are, and she said she'd pay you seventeen dollars an hour to sort through her backlog of packages."

"Really?" I said, intrigued. The pay sounded pretty good for a job that couldn't require too much brainpower. If I worked Sunday afternoons, I'd be more than three hundred dollars a month closer to paying off my always-overdue bills. How hard could it be? Leena's mail counter is only open nine to two on weekdays, so there couldn't be that many boxes stacked in the back room . . . could there?

"Leena said things are a little worse than usual there since she's been focusing on her tomatoes for the past couple months. She's entering San Marzanos in the late-tomato contest next month," Bootsie told me. "Which reminds me, I need the *Heifer in Tomato Patch* story ready to go as soon as Walt gives the okay," Bootsie said, whipping her iPhone from the pocket of her flowered pants.

"Shouldn't you be, like, interviewing Mrs. Potts and some art experts if you're working on a front-page story?" I asked her.

"It's only two. I've got till seven tonight to turn in my story," Bootsie told me. "I usually only need, like, fifteen minutes. I'm an excellent multitasker."

"You could ask George about the importance of *Heifer in Tomato Patch*," I suggested. "He'd be discreet if you told him to keep the theft quiet, and he knows everything about the art world. Maybe he'd even have a theory who took it."

George Fogle is the local liaison for Sotheby's, and went to high school with us. He spends most of his time in New York City these days, but comes back to town frequently to meet with local clients—including Holly, who actually buys things like art and "important jewelry." He's always willing to lend his time and expertise, and even helped my elderly neighbors Hugh and Jimmy Best sell an heirloom ring last spring that turned out to be worth $2.7 million—which enabled them to fix the heating and the roof on their formerly crumbling house, pay off their tab at the country club, and enjoy a very comfortable old age.

"Great idea! Once George starts talking about a painting, he can't stop—which is perfect, because I'll just type everything he says, and my story will be done! Boom!" Bootsie said.

"That's it? I thought you were positive it was either Eula or Gianni who took the painting," I said mildly. "You're going to just let them go about their business today?"

"Of course not," she told me. "Holly's going to be at the country club all day, and so will the Colketts and, presumably, Gianni, since the stabbing didn't do much damage. Holly texted me that Eula said she has a mysterious errand to run today, and won't be over at the club till late afternoon. Which sounds totally suspicious, and is why I'm leaving here in five minutes to find her and follow her."

"I don't see why Eula would want to steal Honey's painting," I told Bootsie, climbing down from my stepladder, moving it slightly to the left and dipping my roller brush into the plastic paint tray. "Eula comes from the kind of family that probably has tons of paintings in gilt frames."

"That's true," agreed Bootsie. "But I think Eula's playing a dia-bolical mind game. She figured Honey would be so devastated by the theft that she'd quit the tomato contest," said Bootsie. "Eula would do anything to win this Early Girl competition tomorrow."

"I guess," I said doubtfully. While Bootsie dialed up George, putting him on speakerphone so she could type copious notes into her phone about the works of Hasley Huntingdon-Mews, I painted and mused on the fact that Bootsie had decided this year to enter the early-tomato game herself.

She'd admitted to me after a few beers at the Pub last week that while she'd planted the actual seeds, she'd then turned over the care and nurturing of her tomato plants to her mom, Kitty Delaney, who's an excellent gardener. Bootsie hadn't seen her own tomato plants since April—but had texted, tweeted, and Insta-grammed pics as she'd dropped them off at the country club this morning, since today was the deadline to enter Early Girls in the competition.

Suddenly, George's painting monologue, still emanating from Bootsie's phone's speaker, caught my attention.

"So let me get this straight—Huntingdon-Mews is suddenly hot in the art world?" Bootsie said, still taking notes.

"Yup," George confirmed. "Another of his pastoral scenes, *Ewe in Sunlit Meadow*, sold last month at auction for two hundred and fifty thousand dollars. That's an all-time high for his work, and represents a hundred and fifty percent increase in value over the past ten years."

Just then, the country club's booziest members, Mr. and Mrs. Bingham, opened the screen door to the shop.

"That old oil painting might be worth three quarters of a million dollars?" Mr. Bingham said, emitting a slightly boozy whistle of admiration at the hefty price tag and adjusting his striped bow tie.

"That kind of money could stock us with white zinfandel for life!" said Mrs. Bingham, looking her usual colorful, cheery self in a coral shift dress, with lipstick to match.

The Binghams, passionate consumers of chilled wine, are a kindly if tipsy pair invariably found eating lunch at the club. I have a soft spot for the Binghams, who smell faintly of soap and mothballs. Mr. Bingham is a retired banker and genial fellow in his late sixties, one of those golf-tanned gents who seemingly never ages, and is in a perpetual good mood. He and his wife have always been around town, seeming completely happy with their gardening and an occasional nine holes of golf for Mr. B.

Because they drink from about 9 a.m. on, they don't make a ton of sense, but they're a likable pair. Unfortunately, they like to repeat newsy items heard around town, but their retelling is invariably full of errors. By the time they got through with George's *Heifer* info, Honey's painting would have been bought by a Russian billionaire or headed for the Louvre to hang next to the *Mona Lisa*.

"Could be!" said Bootsie, adding fuel to the fire. "Check out my front-page story tomorrow for details."

"Speaking of which, there's a *Gazette* story appearing this week in which we play a prominent role," Mrs. Bingham whispered loudly to us with a little wink. "Stay tuned, because you're going to love it.

"We wanted you to write it," she added to Bootsie, "but that little Eula was persistent as the dickens. She's a born reporter. Anyway, love the pink paint!"

As the Binghams left, Sophie burst through the shop's doors, huge sunglasses obscuring most of her small face, and an uncharacteristically dejected slump to her tiny shoulders. She wore a pink Lilly minidress that looked adorable, but all of her usual jewelry and glitzy sandals were missing, along with her usual upbeat attitude.

"Are you okay, Sophie?" I asked her, concerned. "Did you talk to your lawyer yet?" I asked her as she sat down on a little bench by the front window and patted Waffles tentatively as he wagged up at her.

"Yeah, I just came from his office. I've been there since eight this morning!" she said. "I showed him the papers I got handed last night, and he said Barclay's demands are BS. He's just dragging out the divorce to be a jerk! Which is no surprise! Plus my guy knows a paralegal over at Barclay's attorney's office, and he's pretty sure he can bribe him, because this paralegal is saving up for law school and he needs the cash real bad.

"But it's not Barclay who's ruining my life—it's Joe!" she added, and erupted into a huge sob and a storm of tears.

Waffles went running for his dog bed, and Bootsie looked distinctly uncomfortable. Her tennis-playing, vodka-sipping family doesn't do crying. If they're upset, they swim in a lake in Maine and have an extra couple of cocktails.

"I'm sorry," I told Sophie, putting down my paint roller to sit down with her. "You two will work things out. You really love each other!"

"Ya think?" she said, pushing up her sunglasses as a ray of hope dawned on her tear-streaked face. "Because I brought up getting engaged again this morning, and he told me that he couldn't talk about it because the fabric came in wrong for the curtains in our new living room, and it was a fuckup of epic proportions."

"He gets really focused on fabrics!" I told her encouragingly. "That's just how he is. Plus Joe's not a morning person, so maybe you can bring it up again over dinner."

"I know! I mean, all I said was that we should talk about pear-shaped versus emerald-cut engagement rocks, and that I know some guys in Jersey who have incredible discount diamonds, and he grabbed his fabric swatches and took off! Jumped in his car and was gone in, like, 2.3 seconds. It was only seven-forty-five in the morning!" Sophie wailed.

"He probably, um, went to the diner for breakfast, and then to the fabric showroom to straighten out the curtain fuckup," I told her, feeling a wave of sympathy for Sophie—as well as for Joe, who gulps anxiety meds anytime the subject of marriage comes up. "Plus he told me last night he's dying to go over and critique the tent for the Tomato Party. He gets really jealous when the Colketts are doing any high-profile jobs," I added.

"Ya got a point there." Sophie sniffled, dabbing at her eyes with a Starbucks napkin she'd dug out of her Versace bag. "He's real mad that the Colketts got that job, but like I told him, Mrs. Earle paid him out the wazoo to do her kitchen job in Florida, and she wasn't about to let him out of her sight for the last two weeks."

"That's probably why he's so pissy!" I told Sophie.

"That, and he wasn't in the mood for lovin' last night after we saw Gerda," Sophie said. "And then this morning, he said he never should have left town and left Holly to deal with Eula Morris on her own, because he knows exactly how to handle Eula." She paused for a second. "He really hates Eula! It's kinda weird, to be honest."

"It dates back to the senior prom," I told her.

"Speaking of Eula," Bootsie said, "I'm heading out in a minute to trail her movements for the next twelve hours. I'm fairly certain she's going to have to move *Heifer in Tomato Patch* if it's in her house, because Walt will look for it there."

"I'll come with ya!" Sophie told her. "I got nothing else to do, and maybe if Joe misses me, he'll start to appreciate me."

"One thing's for sure, Eula has to get her Early Girls to the club by 6 p.m. today to meet the contest deadline," Bootsie said, getting up and grabbing her tote bag. "Even though her mom probably grew her tomatoes for her."

"That's exactly what you're doing," I told Bootsie, frustrated. "You're taking credit for your mom's Early Girls."

"Whatever." She shrugged. "I already dropped them off this

morning, and I don't mean to brag, but I did a fantastic job for a first-time exhibitor."

"You didn't grow them!"

"Doesn't Eula drive a Miata?" asked Sophie, squinting out the front window of my shop. "Because there's a blue Miata pulling out of the ten-minute parking spot in front of the diner right now, and I think she's behind the wheel."

"Eula's on the move!" screamed Bootsie. "Let's go!"

FORTY-FIVE MINUTES LATER, the Miata exited the Atlantic City expressway at Farmville, N.J., and Eula turned right onto a two-lane road that a rusty sign indicated was Route 192.

All around us were neat fields of squash, lettuce, and—what else?—tomatoes. After following her for several miles at a discreet distance, and letting first a tractor and then a pickup truck turn onto Route 192 between us and Eula, the Miata took another right down a long dusty lane toward a large greenhouse.

Bootsie parked behind a convenient grove of pine trees, concealing her Range Rover, which was no easy feat given that there was still a canoe strapped to the roof. She kept the engine running and the air conditioner at full blast, since the temperature outside was eighty-one and humid.

In the backseat next to me was Waffles, who I'd insisted we take with us. I'd told Bootsie it was because of the paint fumes at The Striped Awning weren't healthy for the dog to breathe, but the truth is that once you get in the car with Bootsie at the wheel, you don't know how long you're going to be gone. Luckily, I'd stopped home at noon to let out John's pack of dogs and had given them a lunchtime snack. I'd have to call Joe or Holly to take the next doggie shift if the Eula stalking took too long, and neither one of them are exactly dog people.

"Luckily, I've got bird-watching binoculars from L.L. Bean sale right here," Bootsie said, ripping open a box she grabbed from the backseat and aiming the lenses at Eula. "I didn't get around to unpacking the car yet."

"I'm real surprised this girl wears beige to schlep plants," observed Sophie. "Her dry-cleaning bill must be through the roof."

Eula took a key out of the pocket of her swoopy beige skirt, and the door swung open. A moment later, she reemerged from the greenhouse, carefully toting a tall, lush plant, staked in its terracotta pot. Even from our spot behind the trees, I could see that the leafy vine was fully loaded with robust red vegetables.

"She's picking up tomato plants!" said Bootsie, outraged, staring through her binoculars, her mouth agape. She dropped the binoculars and grabbed her phone, snapping photos of Eula and her Jersey tomatoes as her nemesis toted the plants out of the greenhouse and into the Miata.

"Those are Early Girls!" screamed Bootsie. "My category! I can't believe she's growing them in Jersey. That's a flagrant violation of rule seven of the Tomato Show. Obviously, any vegetable grown east of the Delaware River is going to win. The soil over here is unbeatable!"

"They don't call it the Garden State for nothin'!" Sophie observed, checking her own phone for about the millionth time since we'd gotten in Bootsie's car. "I can't believe Joe still hasn't texted me."

Just then, Eula locked up the greenhouse, put the top up on her Miata, did a three-point turn, and carefully steered down the bumpy lane and back out onto Route 192. She took a left back toward the expressway, presumably intent on getting her Jersey tomatoes back to the country club by 6 p.m. and never glancing in the direction of our grove of trees.

"I'm starving," announced Bootsie. "I'm trying to decide if I should send these pics of Eula right to the tomato committee, or wait till she wins, and then discredit her right then and there. I need food."

"You finished lunch barely two hours ago," I told Bootsie, who shrugged and told me that her whole family has to eat six meals a day, and that she was protein-loading for an upcoming tennis tournament.

"I'm kinda hungry, too," agreed Sophie. "Look at all these tomato fields around here!" She paused for a second, staring down the road as recognition dawned on her small face.

"You know what, this road looks real familiar," she said. "See that barn with the faded Budweiser logo on it, and that farm stand with the sign in the shape of a chicken?"

We peered down the empty two-lane road, where only the chirp of crickets could be heard in the afternoon sunshine. Down the road, there was indeed a barn, the Bud logo, truckloads of squash and veggies for sale, and the bird-shaped sign.

"I know where we are!" yelped Sophie. "We're less than a mile from the best restaurant in Jersey. Take a left at the giant chicken!"

Chapter 8

"YOU'RE GONNA LOVE Midnight Tony's!" shrieked Sophie three minutes later, as we bounced down the unmarked road she'd indicated.

Suddenly, just past a field of zucchini, a large parking lot and spotlighted structure appeared that would have been right at home on the Vegas Strip. The exterior of the structure featured columns, statues of Zeus and Apollo, and a large fountain near the front door. The music of Michael Bublé was emanating from hidden speakers.

I blinked. Midnight Tony's projected a fun vibe, to be sure, and the parking lot was already close to full at—I consulted my watch—four in the afternoon.

Next to us, a group got out of large BMW sedan with New York plates. All four arrivees were dressed to the nines, the men in sharp-looking dark suits and their wives fully decked out in sexy summer dresses and heels. I looked first at Waffles, who was wagging and drooling next to me, eager to check out the action, and then down at my outfit: khaki shorts and Target tank top.

"I can't go in—this place looks pretty fancy," I told Sophie, self-pity swelling up inside me. "Plus I need to keep the air-conditioning on in the car for Waffles. I'll take him for a walk around the parking lot while you guys grab some food."

"Don't worry!" Sophie told me. "Dogs are welcome at Midnight Tony's! He operates outside most of the standard health and licensing rules, since Tony's friends with tons of politicians. Here," she said, digging inside her gold purse. "I have a caftan in here that I was gonna see if you wanted—it's perfect for ya!"

Two minutes later, I was inside the caftan (which wasn't so easy to wriggle into, even in the roomy backseat of a Range Rover), which was a flowered Lilly Pulitzer number that must have been way too long on Sophie, but just grazed my ankles and had a really cute pink seahorse pattern. Sophie gave me a quick coat of mascara and lip gloss, since she carries a full makeup kit at all times, and we were ready to go.

"This place smells amazing!" crowed Bootsie.

Midnight Tony's was indeed scented with a heady aroma of tomato, garlic, sausage, and rosemary. There was a huge U-shaped bar in the front, with chocolate-hued walls and tiny brass sconces creating a convivial, Rat Packy–style vibe, and a large dining room that included comfy leather-upholstered booths and white-clothed tables behind it. The air-conditioning was on full blast, and customers ranged in age from guys in their twenties all the way up to couples in their eighties, with women in sparkly shoes, guys in suits and sport coats. Cleavage was lavish, and eyelashes were long. A band fronted by a guy in a tuxedo belted out oldies, and the mood was super-festive.

The people who didn't really fit in, to be honest, were me and Bootsie. Every other hemline in the place stopped at mid-thigh, and my caftan was getting strange looks. Bootsie's Talbots golf skirt, polo shirt, and whale-print sandals were even more out of place, as was her makeup-free, sporty vibe. No one seemed to mind, though, that we had a large basset hound with us, wagging at everything in sight.

Plus Sophie was right: Waffles wasn't the only mutt in the place. I saw a Yorkie, a Bichon, a Cavalier King Charles, and several other tiny dogs sitting in the dining room with a group of Real Housewife–style ladies in their forties. Another booth was full of uniformed policemen digging into plates of clams casino, and behind them were a bunch of girls having a bachelorette celebration complete with one wearing a "Bride" sash and a tiara.

"Sophiieeee!" said a man in a crisp white shirt and a beautifully cut suit who rushed toward us, shaking Sophie's hand and emitting a waft of pleasant-smelling cologne. He was tanned and impeccably groomed, and appeared to be in his early sixties. He beamed down at our friend.

"Toooonyyy!" sang Sophie. "I've missed ya!" she added, giving him a double cheek kiss.

"I can't believe it, what's it been, five years?" said Midnight Tony. "And you won't believe it, but guess who's here, too?"

He indicated a dark-haired man at the bar, who was several years younger than Tony, but just as flawlessly bronzed and handsome, and in a cool navy sport coat and dark jeans. He immediately jumped up and enveloped Sophie in a huge hug.

"Lobster Phil LaMonte!" shrieked Sophie. "What are you doing back in Jersey?"

AFTER MIDNIGHT TONY, Lobster Phil, and Sophie had exchanged about five minutes of "You keep getting younger" and "It's been too long" greetings, Tony led us to his best booth, whereupon Phil joined us and insisted he was going to buy us dinner.

"What the hell. Order a petit filet for the doggie, too!" Lobster Phil said, immediately endearing himself to me.

To be honest, I was slightly nervous about dining in an off-the-books restaurant with what could only be some of Sophie and Barclay's former Trenton business associates. Then again, Lobster Phil was clearly a dog lover, so he had to be okay. And if the police were eating here, that made the place perfectly safe—right?

"These are my friends Bootsie and Kristin," Sophie said as Tony seated us on the Naugahyde banquette and waiters immediately delivered Chianti, rustic bread, olive oil, and a huge plate of grilled figs topped with Gorgonzola. "We all live over in Pennsylvania, and this one"—here, she indicated Bootsie—"is, like, a champion eater."

"Luckily, I got a lotta money with me!" joked Phil—at least I thought he was joking, until he whipped out a packet of bills and started tipping every waiter who passed by our table.

"Is that a poker game I see in the back?" Bootsie asked Tony, who was still hovering at our table, as she ripped into the bread. "Because I happen to be an excellent card player."

I knew this to be bullshit—Bootsie's not that good at cards. She's decent at bluffing, but that's about it. I gave her a nervous elbow in the side, mouthing *Be quiet!* at her.

"Poker is for members only," Tony told her smoothly. "Probably it's better if you eat and drink only. Enjoy yourself! I'm going to send out my famous fourteen-layer lasagna!" With that, Tony excused himself.

"Best lasagna on the East Coast!" Lobster Phil promised. "So, Sophie, I heard you moved to a quiet little village somewhere and dumped that deadweight, Barclay. And I hear my old friend Gianni Brunello has a fancy restaurant over in the same town. Whaddaya doing over here in Farmville?" he added.

"We were following someone," Sophie told him. "A pricey painting was stolen from a lady we know, and Bootsie here thinks it was stolen by this girl Eula, who, incidentally, is a real pain in the ass."

"Uh-huh." Phil nodded, as if this all made sense to him. "Is this painting a Monet? A Manet? Some other famous artist?"

"It's by a guy named Hasley Huntingdon-Mews," Bootsie told him. "And it's worth somewhere between one hundred and two hundred and fifty thousand dollars, according to a friend of ours who works at Sotheby's."

Phil's eyebrows shot north. "And this disappeared when?" he asked.

"Yesterday!" Sophie said. "And the police—well, it's *a* police in Bryn Mawr, 'cause there's only one guy in the whole department, unless you count his teenage intern—think maybe someone took this artwork not knowing that the thing's worth a ton of money!"

"I might just look into this a little," Phil told us. "Just in case the painting wasn't stolen by the pain-in-the-ass girl, but by someone more professional. I could maybe help out a little."

"Oh yeah, Phil, you always did like art!" Sophie said, glugging some wine. "If you hear anything that would be a big help to our friend Mrs. Potts."

"I'll send a couple texts," said Phil, then proceeded to tap at his phone while I experienced mild alarm bells. Why would a guy named Lobster Phil care about an old British painting?

Did Vegas crime ties extend into international art theft . . . that had somehow found its way to tiny Bryn Mawr? When he said "help out," did he mean he'd return *Heifer* to Mrs. Potts—or grab it for himself, unload it in Europe or Canada, and pocket two hundred and fifty grand?

"Anyway, we followed Eula over here, but then it turned out she was just picking up tomatoes," Sophie told him. She didn't seem to think Phil's interest in *Heifer* was out of the ordinary. "Turns out she's cheating in a tomato-growing contest."

"Early Girls," Bootsie informed him, as a waiter brought a bowl of chilled water for Waffles, which he happily slurped.

"I hear you," nodded Phil. "There's a lot of tomato fraud in this part of Jersey. Farmville's known for its Sweet 100s and Super-steaks, but the quick-growing varieties are real good around here, too. Midnight Tony uses them in his famous sauce. Wait till you taste it!" he told Bootsie, with an admiring look as she polished off the figs.

"I like your style," he told her. "My ex-girlfriend Diana-Maria could eat like a champ, too. Unfortunately, the girl had no brains! Which is why she's not around anymore," he added bitterly, his genial vibe suddenly gone.

Not around anymore? What did that mean?

With that, Phil got up, excusing himself to go greet a federal judge who'd just walked in, and promising he'd be back in a few minutes.

"Bootsie, eat up and let's go!" I whispered. "Stop asking if you can get in on a card game. Those guys are not people you'd want to win money from unless you want to float up from the bottom of the Delaware River tomorrow morning."

The lasagna and steak arrived as Phil returned, his good mood restored.

"It's great to be back in Jersey!" he told us, giving Sophie's arm an affectionate little squeeze. "I live in Vegas now, but I can't go a whole summer without hitting the beach. I have a suite at Caesar's in A.C. for a couple weeks. You girls should come down and hit the slots with me!"

"What's the story on your nickname?" Bootsie asked as we all dug into the lasagna, which was as decadent as it sounded, and Waffles hoovered up his steak, which had been thoughtfully sliced into basset-friendly bites.

"Phil had a real good seafood spot at the Jersey shore when I was first dating Barclay," Sophie told us. "Steamed, broiled, grilled, you name it, he did it to a lobster. It was awesome."

"We did shrimp and clams, too," Phil told us. "All types of seafood, but ninety percent of my business was lobster. The secret is butter. People told us, 'Oh, I want it plain, too much cholesterol,' yada yada. If you're having lobster, you gotta have butter."

"I hear that," said Bootsie.

"So we agreed with them, but put butter on everything anyway!" Phil told us, pushing aside his lasagna and pouring himself some wine. I noticed that he, like Midnight Tony, smelled excellent, and was so well groomed that his skin actually glowed.

"It was a real fun place with live music and a dock," Sophie explained. "Why'd you close it again, Phil? I never understood! You always had a packed house!"

"Tax misunderstanding," Phil explained. "But you know what, I just opened a new Lobster Phil's in Vegas. We recreated everything down to the salt air misting every ten minutes, we got a dance band, we even have a little mini-boardwalk and deck. Plus there are slot machines. You'd never know you weren't in Jersey!

"So, Sophie, you like living over near Philly?" Lobster Phil asked, turning more serious. "Because you deserve a good life. You're a nice girl."

"I love where I live now, and I have a great new boyfriend—he's a decorator," Sophie told Phil. Then her eyes welled up with tears. "Well, make that *had* a boyfriend. We had a fight. But anyway, the little town where we live is really nice, and there are tons of trees and old houses. It's beautiful!"

Phil looked upset when a tear dropped onto Sophie's cheek. "Yeesh. I didn't mean to make you cry," he told her. "Not that I don't know how you feel," he added consolingly. "I mean, just look at what happened with me and my girlfriend Diana-Maria."

"What *did* happen to her?" asked Sophie, as she blew her nose into a napkin.

"You don't want to know," said Phil. "Anyway, Sophie, give me your number. I'll drive over one day to check out this cute little village you live in now. Maybe find out more about your friend's missing painting, too."

Sophie and Phil exchanged contact info while Bootsie finished my lasagna, and I checked a couple of texts from Holly.

Gianni was at the club on crutches. With the assistance of the Colketts, Gerda was building him a grill-slash-smoker out of a steel drum and some chicken wire. Eula had dropped off her Early Girls. Joe had come to the club at four, spied the margarita machine, plugged it in, and downed half the tank.

Concurrently, I worried about Diana-Maria. Had she disappeared into the bottom of a bay or been cemented into a casino? As I pondered this, a guy came up to the table, eyeing Bootsie with interest.

"How 'bout a dance, hon?" he asked.

Bootsie, who took ballroom lessons with her husband, Will,

before they got married, leaped to her feet, but just then, a text dinged in my phone from Holly that indicated things back home were blowing up.

"Time to go!" I told Sophie and Bootsie. "There's a Colkett crisis at the club."

Chapter 9

"*HEIFER IN TOMATO Patch* is back," said Holly when we walked into the club forty-five minutes later. "Abby went in to Swiffer the Camellia Room, and there it was." She glanced down at Waffles, who wagged up at her and then gave a short woof when Joe appeared from outside. He looked slightly worse for wear: His hands were trembling, and he was clutching a frozen margarita and a cigarette.

"Honey Bunny!" shrieked Sophie, forgetting they were in a fight. "You look awful! Are ya drunk?"

"I've had a few," Joe told her.

"Honey Potts is having a reunion with her painting in the Camellia Room, and the Colketts and Gianni are fighting outside," Holly continued. We all trooped into the small conference room, where Mrs. Potts was standing in front of the canvas, frowning.

"Something's not right," said the heiress gruffly. "I've called George Fogle to look at *Heifer*. Meanwhile, I'm taking her home." With that, she hoisted the hefty frame and canvas, refusing all offers of help, and left.

Dusk had fallen outside, and the scent of hickory smoke wafted from over by the tennis courts, where Gerda was at work, safety goggles in place. As a test drive for the party tomorrow night, the Colketts had lighted the chandeliers dangling from the syca-mores, and lanterns flickered outside the pretty white tent, which was open to the warm summer breeze.

"This is gorgeous!" I told Holly. "The party's going to be amazing!"

Just then, the stern tones of Gerda broke through the festive mood.

"Give me drill and stand back!" she announced sternly. "I almost got this smoker done." She did some power-tooling, and flames erupted from her improvised cooking area.

"Gerda single-handedly built a grill out of a fifty-five-gallon drum today," Holly said airily. "The Colketts have been trying to help, but it hasn't been all that pleasant for them. Gerda's manage-ment style is on the stern side, and the Colketts' strengths lie more in designing parterre gardens and placing chaise lounges."

"We thought Gianni was bad," whispered Tim Colkett, who was headed for the margarita machine. "Gerda is much scarier. I need a Marlboro Silver. What's one more lungful of smoke at this point?"

"Luckily, you just missed Gianni," Holly added. "His pain pills kicked in and he started swaying near the open flame of Gerda's grill, so Abby the waitress is driving him home."

"Holly, I need ride home, too," Gerda announced, apparently done with her grill/smoker project. "I leave those guys Tim and Tom in charge of doing the overnight roasting of the ducks. I'm done for the day, but I come back tomorrow morning at 6 a.m.

"Why is this mutt here?" Gerda added, suddenly taking note of Waffles's adorable freckled body and droopy ears in the faint light from the lanterns. "Is not sanitary to have dogs at a place where people eat. I remember this dog. He's big fatty, needs to lose weight," she helpfully informed me.

Affronted, I opened my mouth to tell her that Waffles was just big-boned, and that in fact, he'd just been welcomed at a fine-dining establishment in Jersey, but instead I decided to leave.

I could tell Bootsie was nowhere near being ready to head home, so Waffles and I would have to walk the two blocks back to The Striped Awning to pick up my car.

"Also, Sophie, don't let this guy drive home," Gerda informed, indicating Joe with her power drill while she packed up her tool box. "He had, like, seven alcoholic drinks."

"Fuck you," Joe told her.

"Bootsie and I will drive everyone home," Holly said, but I was already halfway down the club's driveway by then, having reached my daily fill of arguments and definitely my limit on Gerda. As I passed a slightly dented Mazda, the radio on and the windows down, I noticed two people in it: A girl with long blond hair was in the driver's seat, giggling, while a muscly bald guy was holding her hand and exaggeratedly kissing it.

Gianni and Abby the waitress! She didn't look upset, but then again, a girl in her early twenties isn't prepared for the likes of Gianni and his weird brand of sexiness. Abby needed to head back to college in the fall, not become Gianni's next girlfriend!

I paused for a minute, not sure what to do. I could ask Abby for a ride home, too, and Waffles and I would definitely kill the romantic vibe. I was about to flag Abby down and jump in her backseat when she started up her car, still laughing merrily.

"Hi, Abby!" I called out, and she pulled up next to me. "Are you okay?"

"I'm fine!" she assured me, pointing at the chef, who sometime in the preceding five seconds had fallen asleep and was snoring in the passenger seat, seemingly gone in a Vicodin haze of glory. "Gianni just passed out. I'll take him home and leave him on his front porch!"

Chapter 10

AFTER FIVE HOURS of painting the next morning, Waffles and I decided to make a flea market run to Stoltzfus's, my favorite Amish country antiques hunting ground.

Not only is Stoltzfus's home to acres of outdoor vendors, an indoor barn with additional odds and ends, and a bratwurst stand, it also has my favorite dealers in silver and furniture, Annie and Jenny. There's also a small kiosk selling excellent locally brewed beer, which I try to avoid since the place is only open from 5 a.m. till 2 p.m.

Waffles absolutely loves Stoltzfus's, since Annie and Jenny always give him snacks—although the vegan cruelty-free cookies they bake are so taste-free that Waffles is the only shopper who ever accepts them. As always, the dog emerged from the car determined to gallop to the bratwurst area, then reluctantly agreed to head toward Jenny and Annie's table, where he chewed valiantly on a gluten-free oat bar that seemed resistant to being swallowed. One mighty gulp later, he finally got it down the hatch, and immediately fell asleep in the shade of their van with Jenny giving him a belly rub.

"How are things in Bryn Mawr?" Annie asked me as we exchanged greetings and chatted. "Any church sales coming up? Your town has amazing stuff in its attics!"

"I'll keep you posted," I promised. The stuff that Bryn Mawrians donate to church sales does tend to be pretty awesome, with sets of monogrammed silverware and dessert plates going for ten or fifteen dollars, which I could then polish and sell at The Striped Awning for a significant markup. Annie and Jenny prowled such events all over Pennsylvania, even heading as far as Maine and Vermont in the warmer months.

"We met another girl from your town a few times recently here at the market," Jenny told me, continuing her affectionate doggie rubdown while Waffles gazed up at her ecstatically. "She buys old frames and then paints over the canvases as a hobby, then she brings back the new paintings to sell a couple times a year."

I half listened as I inspected a set of pretty Limoges serving platters.

"She has a deal with the guy who sells the organic corndogs," Jenny went on. "He handles her art sales."

"Her work is pretty cute!" offered Annie. "She does copies of paintings by Old Masters and major artists like Van Gogh. Maybe you know her—little short gal, always wears beige? And low-heeled pumps? Which is kind of weird since everyone else here is in sneakers and flip-flops."

Beige outfits and sensible pumps—from Bryn Mawr? That could only describe one person, because the town just isn't that big.

If Eula was out here buying old paintings, remaking the canvases, and reselling them, could she actually be the culprit in the *Heifer* heist?

Was it possible that Bootsie was actually *right*? Maybe Eula had a weird obsession with valuable paintings! I'd read about art thieves who took paintings just to see if they could, and then locked them in a basement or a barn to molder away.

And who knew that Eula was a skilled copier of famous paintings? What if she stole *Heifer*, and then painted over it for reasons only she understood? Casually destroying paintings might be one of Eula's raisons d'etre, right up there with bossing people around!

She might at this very moment be selling a seven-hundred-thousand-dollar English landscape disguised as, say, Monet's *Water Lilies*, while all around her, shoppers munched blithely on organic corndogs.

"Is that girl in the beige outfits here today?" I asked breathlessly, my mind still running through possible reasons why Eula Morris, an annoying but seemingly law-abiding young woman with a passion for tomato growing and tennis, had taken this unusual turn toward crime.

"I haven't seen her." Annie shrugged. "But I did see those florists you know. Nice guys, really well dressed, always kinda tipsy?"

The Colketts!

I occasionally run into them at Stoltzfus's, which I never expect. The Colketts are super-upscale, and Stoltzfus's isn't. But they sometimes buy old garden benches or topiary forms here, and it's near their greenhouses, where they have gardeners raising the buoyant roses and hydrangeas their customers love.

Anyway, the Colketts would definitely have noticed if Eula had been here today—well, they *probably* would have noticed.

I mean, the painting was fairly large, and Eula is fairly small, so she would have been noticeable if she was schlepping the hefty framed canvas through the mass of vendors. Then again, the

Colketts might have been distracted by the indoor beer stand and completely missed Eula.

I bought a pretty footed tray and a little silver-plated candy dish from Annie and Jenny for a total of twenty-two dollars. Then Waffles and I waved good-bye and went in search of Eula and/or the Colketts.

I FOUND TIM and Tom heading out from the beer area to their white paneled truck, looking somewhat out of place with the rumpled hordes—including Waffles and myself—at Stoltzfus's.

Like Joe and Holly, the Colketts are invariably impeccable. Somehow, their clothes refuse to wrinkle or attract dust no matter what they do, and both wore well-cut khakis and polo shirts. As always, they smelled amazingly clean and citrusy, and greeted me and Waffles pleasantly enough, emitting a faint whiff of pilsner when they gave me their standard cheek-kiss greeting. Not surprisingly, they looked a bit worn from their party preparations, and they also looked like they were in a hurry.

This struck me as odd, since the Colketts have a special talent for the pleasantries of life—they accomplish a lot, but always seem to have time to pause and exchange a little gossip.

Today, though, Tom hustled to slam the rear doors of the truck closed, then made a beeline for the passenger door, while Tim headed for the driver's seat, keys at the ready.

"How are you guys?" I asked. "Have you recovered from dealing with Gerda and Chef Gianni yesterday?"

"Honestly, doll, we'd like to change our identities and move to Peru to get away from the two of them, but that Food Network contract pays so much that we can't," Tom said.

"I never thought that getting the feathers off forty-five ducks and then slow-roasting them over a 210-degree flame could take so much out of a person," agreed Tim. "We had to nap in shifts all night and take turns basting."

"That sounds awful," I agreed, truthfully. "By the way, you haven't seen Eula Morris out here at the flea market, have you?"

"No, thankfully," said Tim. I briefly explained Annie and Jenny had met Eula here recently.

"Weird," agreed Tom. "I mean, Eula pops up a lot of times just when you don't want her, but I can't picture her here amid this crazy scene!" He gestured at the motley group of vendors and shoppers around us.

"She doesn't strike me as the road-trip type," Tim seconded.

"Eula might surprise you," I told them. She'd definitely shocked me in the past couple days with her secret New Jersey tomato greenhouse and her side business of art forging.

"I'm still recovering from her Tuscan farm theme idea," Tom said, jumping into the passenger seat. "Anyway, doll, see you at the club tonight. We've got a truckload of hydrangeas that can't sit here in the heat." With that, the Colketts were gone. They'd seemed genuinely disinterested in Eula and her passion for the paintbrush.

Were the Colketts up to something painting-related? Or were they just embarrassed to be caught mid-pilsner when their big event was less than four hours away from welcoming the tomato-obsessed of our town? If so, I certainly wasn't judging them. They'd done an amazing job designing the party. Plus months of dealing with Gianni and a single day of Gerda would drive anyone to drink.

I sighed as Waffles and I got into the car and cranked up the air-conditioning.

If only John hadn't gone to that vet clinic, he might be here with me, since he was the kind of guy willing to help his girlfriend schlep antiques. John was amazing—and Mike Woodford wasn't, I reminded myself! As soon as John was back in town, I was steering clear of Bootsie and her schemes, and any talk of missing paintings.

Before I steered away from the flea market crowds, though, I made two calls. First, I reached Walt at the Bryn Mawr Police Station and relayed what Annie and Jenny had told me about Eula's painting skills—it didn't seem relevant, but I thought Walt should know. Then, naturally, I called Bootsie.

Chapter 11

THE NIGHT WAS perfect for the Tomato Party, with a light breeze ruffling the sycamores, and the temperature in the low seventies. I heard the whir of the margarita machine, and felt a surge of gratitude to Holly.

Thanks to her generosity, I was once again a guest at a party I couldn't afford, and gave her a little hug when I arrived at five-thirty, an hour before the party was due to start.

As party co-chair and sponsor, Holly had handed us all free tickets for tonight's event, and had delivered a pink silk Trina Turk dress to me with strict orders to wear it. As always, she claimed it was headed for a Goodwill drop-off—which was possibly true, since Holly has a shopping problem. She buys a ton of stuff that she later decides "makes her look like a couch." Also, since Leena at the Pack-N-Ship is known for losing packages, the returns that Holly tries to mail back rarely get there.

Holly had to be desperate for this party to finally happen—and end. It had taken over her entire summer, and sent her husband, Howard, to buy up a trash and trucking company in Oregon, since he told Holly it was better for everyone if he left town until she was done with the event.

"The tent looks amazing!" I told Holly, and in fact, the setting was truly gorgeous. The red-and-white chevron floor lent a chic air to the party space, and huge glass vases filled with tomatoes of every type sat on sleek glass shelves behind the white lacquer bar. "Tomatoes have never looked so cool!"

"It's amazing what the Colketts can do with three thousand votive candles, twelve thousand dollars' worth of orchids, and twenty-seven rented Venetian chandeliers," said Holly, smiling sweetly at the designers.

"We honestly are so talented that even we can't believe it sometimes!" Tim agreed tipsily. "Thank goodness Gianni got that TV show so our genius can reach a wider audience. I just hope this country-club crowd appreciates us. Speaking of which, where's Eula?"

"I sent her to go supervise Gianni." Holly snickered. "That should go well."

Holly quickly explained that Gianni and Skipper had set up separate rival areas on which to stage their hors d'oeuvres. Gianni's moulard birds were currently sending up savory scents as they sizzled above a wood-burning temporary grill.

Nearby, screened by some potted plants, a tiny figure in black was grimly rolling out dough on a long wooden table, which she then cut into long strands and handed over to a guy who plunged them into a giant pot of water boiling over a portable stove.

"Ugh, there's Gianni's granny, or whoever she is." Tim shuddered, nudging Tom. "Look, Tom, it's Nonna Claudia! And she's as ghoulish as ever!" he added, giving the lady a little wave, which she ignored.

"She scares us," Tom whispered to me and Holly with a little shudder. "When she was out in Beverly Hills training the kitchen staff, it was like, we need to move up cocktail hour from 10 a.m. to 9 a.m. just to deal with her sourpuss face! Never a smile, not even once!"

"I've seen her before somewhere," said Holly, with a little frown of concentration. "She looks so familiar."

"She works at Ristorante Gianni," I told her. "You probably saw her coming out of the kitchen and heading upstairs the other night."

"Which is totally sinister," sang out Tim Colkett. "I mean, just think, she and her cat are upstairs all the time, watching the parking lot and, like, judging people's outfits when they walk in to dinner!"

"Gianni wants all the credit for his feather light pasta for himself, but of course we know it's all her. I mean, she was in L.A. for three weeks at the new restaurant training the pasta chefs, but she never talked to us once. The weird part is that the Food Network people said she made great TV!" Tom told us. "They were super-bummed when she packed up her pasta machine and told Gianni she was coming back here.

"Anyway," he added, "did you notice we stealthily incorporated four hundred branches of tiny tomato blossoms around the entrance to the tent? Trust me, that was a huge argument with a farmer in Delaware. And it was worth the battle we had to personally select them this morning and truck them up here this afternoon!"

I had to agree, though truthfully, I wasn't sure that tomato fans such as Mrs. Potts and the Binghams would love the massive installation of yellow tomato flowers created by the Colketts. To this crowd, each of those flowers represented a lost tomato never to be chopped, simmered, and turned into spaghetti sauce.

Just then, I noticed a small band of ladies in Talbots dresses arriving onto the club porch and heading for the tent. I checked my watch—6:05. In true Bryn Mawr tradition, the tomato crowd was almost thirty minutes early for the kickoff party.

For his part, Skipper had stuck with a tried-and-true favorite: He'd gone with a mojito-burrito buffet, a popular combination of items which he'd inaugurated at the country club when he became executive chef last year. Mojito-Burrito Night, while met with some initial resistance from the older members, was now a huge hit at the club and quite affordable at just $9.95.

It's one of the few club events that fits in my meager budget. Actually, I can't afford the club at all, and there's no chance I could pay my annual membership fee, given that I'm behind on rent at the shop and AmEx has been calling my house incessantly about my past due charges. Somehow, though, my club dues are fully up-to-date—Ronnie insists that my grandparents prepaid my fees for several years in advance, but I know it had to have been Holly.

"Where's Eula?" asked Bootsie, popping up at my elbow. She looked very pretty tonight, I noticed, in her standard party outfit of Talbots cotton shift dress and flat sandals. She'd added some dangly earrings, and even gone for a swipe of pink lipstick.

"I've got a plan to get her drunk, then drive her home and search the parts of her house that I couldn't see when I was in her tree on Thursday," Bootsie said. "I did a little legwork outside her house today. It's one story, but there's an attic, and it looks like she's got a secret painting studio up there. I aimed my binoculars at her second floor window, and I'm pretty sure I saw an easel!"

Just then, Sophie and Joe showed up, and I quickly told them about Eula's surprising hobby of selling paintings at Stoltzfus's. Naturally, Joe agreed with Bootsie that Eula was the mastermind behind the *Heifer* heist.

"Where's Gerda?" I asked, hoping she might be skipping the party.

"We just dropped her off at Barclay's place," Sophie told me, wriggling nervously in a silk caftan, while Joe headed for the bar. "She's going to work on figuring out his new e-mail password tonight."

"Hey, everyone," shouted Chef Gianni, limping out from his outdoor kitchen area while three waiters followed him bearing trays of delicious-smelling tiny plates of pasta. The chef waved his crutch for emphasis as a crowd of arriving guests paused, gazing admiringly and sniffing the air. "My duck ragout is finally ready! Gianni got stabbed, but he don't give up!"

Waiters began passing the little plates of pasta to guests, along with tiny silver forks and linen napkins. More servers followed, bearing glasses of some delicious-looking red wine, and Gianni personally helped hand out the snacks to the little crowd of early party guests, doling out kisses to the ladies and doing some greetings of the back-slapping variety to husbands.

I instantly forgot the fact that I don't eat duck, and dug in. The food was so delicious that the group actually cheered.

"Gianni try to be modest, but I killing it with this pasta!" the chef said.

Then he indicated Skipper's burrito setup, which did look a little flat next to Gianni's modern-Italian tour de force. Gianni made a skeptical face as Abby and two other waitresses loading up trays with Skipper's mini-tacos and tiny shrimp tostados.

"I feel like I'm at, what you call it, Taco Bell!" yelled Gianni to the admiring crowd of club members. "What is this, Skipper, refried beans? Maybe I'm at Chipotle!"

"These are organic black beans sautéed in a chili oil, and we have some heirloom tomatoes and fresh cilantro that we grew ourselves in the club's veggie garden. Of course, we make our own tortillas, and the meats are free-range chicken and grass-fed beef . . ."

Skipper wiped some sweat from his brow.

Just then, a huge sheepdog ran up to the gas grill where Skipper and his team were basting a hefty piece of beef. Skipper's signature burrito filling, a flank steak, had floated its smoky, yummy scent out past the sycamores and the laurel hedges, and the sheepdog sat down by the grill, panting and slobbering.

I knew this dog: It was Toby, the Binghams' free-roaming mutt, who enjoys a fence-free existence, but is luckily quite streetwise. Toby pauses at crosswalks and waits at stop signs, so he makes his way around town without incident.

Toby usually respects sheepdog-a non grata zones such as the club, the cow pastures at Sanderson, and the cemetery. But Skipper's flank steak had put this well-mannered pooch over the edge.

"Skipper, your steak brought in a new customer, and he got four legs and a tail!" Gianni shouted to the small crowd of guests. "Hey, don't worry, we all gotta start somewhere!"

"Oh, Toby, you naughty boy," said Mr. Bingham, wandering over in a yellow sport coat, glass of white zinfandel in hand. He waved a finger at his wayward dog, who merely wagged up at him and kept drooling.

Just then, two yellow Labs showed up, joined Toby grill-side, and commenced whining, while Gianni, earrings gleaming as he leaned on his crutches, kept up a running commentary. "These dogs might hire you for their next party, Skipper! Could be whole new business for you!"

"Bootsie, aren't those your Labs?" I hissed, giving her a nudge.

"Huh—that *is* Chewy and Rocky!" she said, seemingly undisturbed by her dogs having galloped a half mile away from home. "I told Will to make sure our fence got repaired this week. I'll have to call him to come pick them up."

While Bootsie shrugged and dialed her husband, Gianni made a last dig at the club's head chef. "Hey, Skipper, maybe you the one stole that painting of the cow yesterday! You probably need the money."

With this, Skipper had had enough of Gianni. He stalked inside the club and disappeared as the rest of the guests arrived.

"THE PAINTING THAT was returned yesterday is a fake *Heifer in Tomato Patch*," Mrs. Potts told us five minutes later. She downed a mini-taco in one bite, and sipped a large vodka.

"It was almost immediately apparent, though the counterfeit painting was a pretty good one at first glance," confirmed George Fogle, who'd accompanied Honey to the party. The two had spent the day researching forgers of Henry Huntingdon-Mews's works, of which there had been many back in the painter's own century, but none that were known in present-day art circles.

"This version of *Heifer* wasn't painted all that long ago," said George. "Probably earlier this year, since oil paint can take months to fully set onto a canvas. Also, it was layered over an existing canvas. It's a commonly done technique that's called pentimento, this kind of reuse for an old painting. In this case, the artist found a gilt frame and canvas that's almost exactly the size of Honey's original."

A new painting layered atop an old one? Bootsie and I stared at each other.

Eula was a pentimento painter! At least, according to Annie and Jenny. We needed to call Walt.

"That's just like *The Thomas Crown Affair*!" shrieked Sophie. "I love that movie! I mean, when Pierce Brosnan and Rene Russo get naked on his staircase, it's awesome. Although I couldn't stop thinking that cold marble stairs would really hurt your tush."

"It's hard to know if this was supposed to be a joke, or if the artist set out to create a convincing forgery of *Heifer*," continued George. "I made some calls today, and Walt took the fake painting in to try to lift any fingerprints that might have been left. Meanwhile, though, the real painting is still missing."

I told George about Eula's hobby of re-making old canvases, then wondered if this would be a good time to mention to George and Mrs. Potts that a Vegas restaurateur named Lobster Phil LaMonte was also checking around for her painting. Probably not, I decided. It seemed a little too complicated to explain over a mini-taco.

Plus George can be a bit competitive, plus I had a feeling he and Lobster Phil moved in very different circles. And who knows? Let each of them do their own thing, and maybe somewhere between Vegas, Jersey, and the fancy New York art world, one of the two might actually find the wayward canvas.

"Now that I'm done with this party project and I don't have to deal with that hideous Eula Morris," said Holly, "I'm going to devote ninety-three percent of my time to taking you out for cocktails and tracking down your painting, Mrs. P."

Mrs. Potts gave Holly a smile, cheering up a little. Holly's the only person who ever convinced the elderly heiress to wear lip gloss and occasionally put on a tasteful sheath dress instead of her usual Bermuda shorts, and they have an unlikely but firm friendship.

"What are you going to do with the other seven percent of your waking hours?" George asked Holly.

"First, I'm going to get Eula Morris to stop wearing beige, and then I'll come up with a plan to get her to move at least three states away from here!"

TWENTY MINUTES LATER, I wondered if Holly would mind if I took off from the tomato fest. Then again, the ticket she'd generously bought me had been close to one hundred dollars, there was an open bar, and I had on the borrowed Trina Turk dress. But the conversations at this soiree were honestly a little strange.

"I talk to my tomato seeds during the winter," Mrs. Bingham was telling me and Sophie, as her husband gallantly handed her a fresh white zinfandel. I noticed his striped bow tie had slipped to a jaunty angle, and Toby the dog had joined them at the party, still wagging politely at passing guests.

"Uh-huh," said Sophie. "What kind of stuff do ya tell them?"

"I tell them they're destined for greatness!" Mrs. Bingham said with a giggle.

"That, or to be sliced up and served with mozzarella and basil," whispered Tim Colkett.

"Keep talking," said Jimmy Best, my grouchy next-door neighbor, to Mrs. Bingham. "You drink enough, your plants might start answering you."

"I think I have a real shot this year at getting first place in the Mighty Sweets," Mrs. Bingham replied. "I did some new composting, and my babies are the best they've ever been!"

"Mummy gave me some great tips," Bootsie said. "For one, she spritzes everything with vodka. Keeps away the beetles. That, and she uses a ton of Miracle-Gro."

"You ain't allowed to use Miracle-Gro on competition veggies," Jimmy informed her. "No chemicals. I guess vodka's okay, though."

"Hey, isn't that the cute guy you make out with sometimes over there?" Sophie added, giving me a little elbow nudge and nodding in the direction of the tomato display.

Mike Woodford was sipping a vodka drink and inspecting the Early Girl plants alongside his aunt Honey Potts.

"That's him," I confirmed, noting that Mike was in his standard party attire of navy blazer and khakis, along with some brown Gucci loafers. To be honest, Mike looks better when he's in jeans and a T-shirt, but he still looked very cute.

"He's a hot guy!" Sophie said, giving me a little wink.

"But just look at him with those tomatoes—he's more interested in them than he is in talking to me," I told her. Mike was currently bent over what a placard indicated was Eula Morris's plant, looking absolutely fascinated by the glossy red veggies that hung from the slender green stalks. He and Honey were engaged in whispered conversation over the plant with the intensity most people reserve for juicy gossip, not juicy produce.

I tried not to notice the dark beard scruff I found so irresistible on Mike, as he talked animatedly with his aunt. Also, I ignored his deep tan, dark brown eyes, and long lashes, and suppressed the memory of that time we made out in the back room at The Striped Awning . . .

Wait! I was dating John, I told myself sternly. Who was *also* tan, handsome, and actually called me, and spent time with me on a regular basis! Well, usually he did, when he wasn't away at veterinary clinics.

"You know," Bootsie said, interrupting my reverie, "Mike's on my list of suspects for Honey's painting."

"Mike's her nephew, isn't he?" squeaked Sophie. "And, like, her favorite person in the world. He's gonna inherit everything, so he's got no reason to steal it."

"Maybe he needs cash right now," Bootsie told us. "I mean, I hope it was Eula who took *Heifer*, but it could have been Mike. He probably read about that sale of the seven-hundred-thousand-dollar Huntingdon-Mews and decided to grab it, sell it, and speed up his inheritance!"

I considered Bootsie's latest theory for a moment while perching on a bar stool, since Holly's wedge sandals were starting to pinch my toes. In Agatha Christie novels, impatient heirs are always trying to either steal from their own family members or—and this I couldn't even contemplate vis-à-vis Mike Woodford—poison wealthy relatives and accelerate the process of getting their hands on what was listed in a will as rightfully theirs.

But Mike had never shown any interest—other than those Gucci loafers he busts out for parties—in the fancy side of life. Like Honey, he only cares about cows. Plus he already lives on the gorgeous grounds of Sanderson in a fantastic little stone cottage.

"I'm pretty sure the only thing Mike reads is *Organic Farming*," I informed Bootsie. "They probably didn't cover that auction where the other Huntingdon-Mews sold for big bucks."

"I thought you were positive it was either Eula or Gianni who took that piece of art!" added Sophie.

"It's probably Eula or Gianni," agreed Bootsie. "Which is why my plan is to get Eula drunk and then ransack her attic. Wish me luck!"

At that moment, Holly announced that she was ready to head home.

"You've just spent three months and twenty-five thousand dollars of Howard's money on this party, and you're leaving after forty-five minutes?" said Bootsie.

"My work is done," Holly told her. "I wanted to support Mrs. Potts and her passion for the traditional."

"I thought you just wanted to stick it to Eula Morris by taking over the party," Joe pointed out.

"That, too," agreed Holly. "Also, I might be in an existential crisis about whether tomatoes matter."

"So, like, you're searching for the meaning of life?" Sophie asked.

"Not really," Holly told her. "More just for the meaning of the past ninety days I spent planning this dumb party."

"Ya need a sign!" Sophie told her. "I'm a big believer in stuff like messages and signs! I mean, look at how I met Gerda. I saw what I thought was the sign for a Versace boutique across a canal in Venice, and was leaning over to get a better look, and almost fell in the water—and Gerda yanked me out! We've been friends ever since!"

Just then, a blindingly bright light flooded the tent. As a bewildered buzz rose from the guests, and everyone rushed outside.

A huge billboard was visible beyond some trees and just past the first golf tee, its border a Vegas-style line of flashing bulbs.

In huge white letters, the sign read, "Mega Wine Mart! Opening Next Month with 40,000 Square Feet of Discount Booze!"

Chapter 12

WITH THAT, WE all agreed it was time to leave, and went to the Bryn Mawr Pub.

"That Wine Mart has to be your ex's idea," Bootsie told Sophie. "It's exactly the kind of thing he would do."

"It better not be!" Sophie said, stamping her tiny bejeweled spiky heel as we slid into the large booth at the front of the pub. "'Cause if he owns it, I get half of it in the divorce! I gotta go call my lawyer."

"How did you plan a party for three months and not notice that sign going up behind the eighteenth golf green?" Joe asked Holly.

"When Eula's around, I don't have time to look up," she told him.

"My lawyer's gonna look into this new store," Sophie told us, looking up from a text. "He's turned up a bunch a stuff Barclay owns but didn't list in his property accounting."

"I'll find out who's behind the Wine Mart," Bootsie promised. "I'm not going to let Eula steal this story from me!"

"She already did," Joe informed her, holding up his phone, on which he'd brought up a recent *Bryn Mawr Gazette* piece about a new wine store coming to town—which none of us had noticed in the last issue.

"How dare she!" screamed Bootsie. "I cover alcohol-related events!"

"You're supposed to be the town's preeminent reporter," Joe reminded Bootsie. "How did you not know that something called a Mega Wine Mart was being built right off the town's main shopping street?"

"I was in Maine this week," said Bootsie angrily, then calmed down a little. "Although, come to think of it, I might have heard something about a new liquor store. It wasn't a superstore, though."

I was facing the street in our booth, and just then, my attention was caught by a tall, willowy figure that had just wafted through the slightly dingy front door of the Pub.

The lighting was dim in here, emanating from neon beer signs and a Phillies game on a TV above the bar, but after blinking a few times, I knew with a sinking feeling that my first impression had been correct.

The slim and perfect blond girl up near the Pub's all-you-can-eat barrel of peanuts was none other than Lilly Merriwether.

IF ANYTHING, LILLY—who happens to be the ex-wife of my boyfriend, John, and honestly is everything you wouldn't want your boyfriend's ex to be—had gotten better-looking over the past year. Instead of the tennis outfits I'd always seen her in when she was in Bryn Mawr full-time, she wore a really cool-looking, flowy print dress with a halter neck, plus some chic suede sandals.

I gave a little nudge to Holly, and Sophie and Bootsie turned to gaze openmouthed at Lilly, too.

Luckily, Holly isn't a big fan of Lilly's, either. Some of this was out of loyalty to me, since everyone knows you're not supposed to be friendly to a girl who was married to your friend's boyfriend.

Mostly, though, it was because Lilly was Holly's main competition in the gorgeous, slim, and wealthy blond category of girls in town when she lived here.

"Lilly's got on the Thakoon dress I ordered last month," noted Holly coolly. "Luckily, the Pack-N-Ship lost the package, because that dress will never be worn by me now."

"I love her sandals!" said Sophie. "Those are the Aquazzura platform suede ones that tie in the front, I just ordered 'em! They cost, like, seven hundred bucks!"

This news reminded me, with a tiny spark of hope, that Lilly was now living with the tennis-loving scion of a banking family up in Connecticut.

Between Lilly's own family's assets and the tennis guy's cash, maybe she'd focus on fancy shoes, and forget about her ex, John Hall! John's not a pricey sandal kind of guy, thank goodness, so if Lilly was becoming a fashionista on par with Holly and Sophie, she'd be way better off with her banker.

Unfortunately, Bootsie's always been on good terms with Lilly, since they're both weirdly devoted to tennis. She waved Lilly down with a friendly hello, and Lilly floated our way, greeting us all in her sweet-natured voice. Another of the super-annoying things about her is that she's by all accounts a nice person—even John says so, and he's divorced from her.

"How's your mom?" asked Sophie, bringing up the one subject I was desperately hoping to avoid.

When crime had broken out in Bryn Mawr last spring, with Barclay Shields getting attacked with a heavy silver bookend and Gianni getting shot on Holly's patio, Lilly's mom, Mariellen, had turned out to be the culprit.

This had shocked everyone, because while not exactly warm and fuzzy, Mariellen didn't seem like the criminal type. Mariellen's main interest had been her handsome chestnut horse, Norman, until she'd decided that people like Barclay and Gianni were ruining her beloved Bryn Mawr.

Then, after trying to kill Barclay and Gianni, she'd turned her anger toward me for dating John, her ex-son-in-law.

This had seemed unfair, since Lilly and John had separated two years before I'd ever met him, but Mariellen isn't the kind of lady you have a reasonable discussion with over, say, a bowl of chips and salsa. Anyway, after kidnapping me, Waffles, and my neighbors Hugh and Jimmy Best at gunpoint, Mariellen was now living in a ritzy sanitarium within a quick drive of Lilly's new digs in Greenwich.

Which was exactly where they both should be! Far away from Bryn Mawr!

"Mummy's doing great," Lilly said, in an upbeat tone I had to admire. "She and Norman are loving their new home!

"I'm supposed to be meeting a friend here," added Lilly. "Oh, there she is now!" With this, she turned on her pricey heel, and ran over to hug the short girl who'd just flung open the Pub door. We did a group eye roll, because the person Lilly had enveloped in a happy embrace was none other than Eula Morris.

"HEY, EULA." BOOTSIE beckoned her over. "What's up with that billboard and the new wine store? Because your *Gazette* story says nothing about a forty-thousand-square-foot big box store."

"I was told something completely different," Eula said defensively. "Anyway, it was my first assignment for the *Gazette*. I mean, nobody's perfect."

"You did a shitty job, Eula," Joe informed her, waving his phone with the story in question up on his home screen. "You wrote a story about a charming cottage turned French wine store."

"Fuck you, Joe!" Eula told him. "That's what the press release said. I have it right here." She rummaged around in her tote bag and pulled out a sheet of paper.

"See?" she said, shoving it over to Joe, who began to read the two-sided press release, which was headed up by a script-y logo reading "Maison de Booze," and pictured an adorable ivy-covered building set in the woods and surrounded by roses.

"'Formerly the late Mrs. Caroline Bingham's garden store, which closed fifteen years ago,'" read Joe, "'Maison de Booze will offer the best in Beaujolais and other reasonably priced bottles . . . and host free wine and cheese tastings every Thursday and Saturday afternoons . . . in a rustic eighteen-hundred-square-foot setting where all will be welcome to sit and sip at our adorable café tables.'"

"That sounds kind of awesome," said Bootsie, forgetting that she was pissed at Eula. "I guess that's what the Binghams meant yesterday when they told us they were going to be mentioned in the *Gazette* this week. Old Mrs. Bingham's store was a total town landmark back in the day."

"Which is just what I wrote!" said Eula triumphantly. "That the old shop was being turned into this cute Maison de Booze place."

"You missed the second page of the press release," Joe informed her. He'd flipped the release over. "On the back, it says that Maison de Booze will be torn down in eight weeks to make room for the Mega Wine Mart."

Chapter 13

"Does anyone else think Lilly Merriwether might have stolen Honey's painting?" asked Holly. It was eight-forty-five the next morning, and the scent of roses lingered above Holly's outdoor living room, mingling with the fragrance of coffee and freshly mown grass.

"Other than her mom being a homicidal maniac, and the fact that she was married to your boyfriend, I've always liked Lilly." Bootsie shrugged. She'd just arrived and was heading toward a breakfast buffet that Holly's housekeeper had thoughtfully assembled.

"I think Lilly being an unlikely art thief makes perfect sense," Holly continued, ignoring Bootsie. "Plus Lilly getting arrested would be even better than if Gianni or Eula took *Heifer in Tomato Patch*. Not that I'd mind seeing either of them end up in a minimum-security upstate, but it would be even better if Lilly stole it."

I looked up from my plate of Martha's fluffy scrambled eggs, fork frozen in mid-air as joy surged through me. Admiration for

Holly filled my core as I looked at her seemingly serene blue eyes and perfect cheekbones.

Now, this was a loyal friend—one who imagined the worst of your boyfriend's ex!

I gave Bootsie a significant glance indicating my approval of what Holly had just outlined, but Bootsie was busy piling a bagel with a mountain of smoked salmon, eggs, and sliced onions, and missed my daggerlike glare.

"Who knows the exact day when Lilly slunk back into town," Holly added. "She *could* have been back on Thursday, snuck into the club, and taken the painting out that back door by the locker rooms."

"Maybe Lilly grabbed one of the club polo shirts and stabbed Gianni, too," Joe theorized. "Hey—her mom shot him in the leg last year on this very patio. She could have convinced Lilly to try to finish the job."

We all tried to picture the elegant Lilly in an ugly green polo shirt—and failed. Lilly is basically Maria Sharapova, so it's impossible that she'd wear boxy regulation clothes. Ralph Lauren tennis dress, yes; unflattering garments, no.

"I'm pretty sure Lilly's just in town for the annual doubles tournament," Bootsie told us, biting into her bagel sandwich.

"Of course, she's going to have an excuse for coming back—the tennis thing's probably bullshit!" said Joe. "Lilly and Eula could be in it together! Since Lilly's too gorgeous to sneak into the club without anyone noticing, maybe she, like, backed up her car to a side entrance Thursday, and Eula inserted said artwork into her trunk!"

I put my plate of half-eaten eggs onto a cute pouf upholstered in chic pink Moroccan fabric, from which Waffles quickly hoovered the rest of my breakfast.

I had only met Lilly a few times over the years, but had seen her around town fairly often before she'd moved to Greenwich, and there was nothing about her that whispered *burglar*. She was more the type who'd return lost wallets and shovel her elderly neighbors' walkways when it snowed. (Well, probably she'd hire someone else to shovel their walkways, but you get the picture.) I'd even noticed her buying the town firemen a round of beers last night. I sighed.

"As much as I'd like to think of Lilly as potential art smuggler, I don't think she did it." I sighed, dispirited. "For one thing, Lilly's super wealthy, plus her new boyfriend owns a bank or something. And I'm pretty sure she's, well, kind and generous."

"Not if she's friends with Eula!" screamed Joe. He wore a crazed, deer-in-the-headlights expression, perhaps because Sophie was surrounded by a pile of wedding magazines, and was paging through *Town & Country* and turning down corners on all the pages featuring diamonds, which was almost all of them.

"This would be good, Honey Bunny!" she said to Joe, running over to his lounge chair and pointing to a ring the size of a jumbo cocktail olive. "Or this one, which is close to the Liz Taylor diamond from that guy she married twice!"

"Sophie, Joe's a decorator, not Prince Harry," Holly intervened. "Plus he's very understated," she added tactfully, "and he'd pick something more appropriate. You're only four-eleven."

"Liz Taylor was tiny, and she wore huge rocks!" Sophie told her. "It doesn't have to be tasteful. I don't want tasteful."

"You know, there's a Mega Wine Mart up near the L.L. Bean Outlet in Maine," said Bootsie, thankfully changing the subject. "And it's awesome. People come from for Brie and Beaujolais Night, which is, like, every week. A couple times a month, they have French winemakers on-site, and then they pour the *really* good stuff."

"I think that's how Mega Wine Mart is going to get Bryn Mawr Town Council to go along with their store," Joe said. "They laid it out in that fine print in that press release Eula didn't read. Basically, they get us all hooked on the free wine and cheese every Thursday and Saturday at the Maison de Booze in the old garden store. Then, once they put up the megastore, they're going to keep Maison de Booze as a super-pricey wine boutique in a fancy back room of the superstore."

"That's a huge trend right now in retail," Sophie piped up. "The store-within-a-store concept. Like when Lilly P. did their collection for Target. Gerda and I went to the Target over by the mall at 5 a.m. the day it went on sale, but it was all gone in six minutes!"

"Wait a minute—you think people will vote yes to tearing down old Mrs. Bingham's adorable garden store, and uprooting, like, five thousand oak trees and wild rosebushes in the woods there, and, you know, forcing squirrels to flee the forest when they put up some huge concrete warehouse . . . just because they're going to get free Havarti?" Holly asked.

"Of *course* people are gonna go for the free cheese," Joe said, staring at Holly, dumbfounded that she would even consider the alternative.

"I would," I admitted. Honestly, wine and cheese are pricey, and the Mega Wine Mart sounded like it would be serving wines I could never afford.

If I hung out long enough and chugged down my fair share of the gratis Kendall-Jackson, my Progresso soup dinners would seem a lot better, too. "I'd do almost anything for free wine and cheese," I added truthfully.

"Me too," said Bootsie. "Please—the entire town will be there. If they have, say, crackers and salami along with the cheese, and maybe throw in some veggies and dip on the side, that's dinner. And you *know* everyone's going to go for that."

"I love free stuff!" agreed Sophie. "I'll go!"

"You're the only person in the whole tri-state region who won't be there," Joe informed Holly. "But that doesn't mean that Mega Wine Mart should be allowed to, you know, desecrate the forest. In theory, I'm against it."

"Don't listen to Holly! She doesn't even eat cheese," Bootsie argued, then thought for a moment. "I guess I'm against the superstore, but I'd love to have that Maison de Booze."

"I think there's a way we can get the free wine and cheese, and keep the trees and squirrels," Joe said.

"I'm scared of squirrels!" Sophie announced.

"I think I see where you're going with this," Bootsie said to Joe. "Derail the megastore, but convince the owners that we need the Maison de Booze."

"Exactly," he agreed. "Since Mega Wine Marts are independently owned franchises, we need to figure out who's opening this store. Weirdly, though, there's nothing coming up on the Internet about who's behind the Bryn Mawr location.

"I called the Binghams at 8:30 a.m., since obviously they'll know who bought his mom's old shop, but they didn't answer at their house, and people like that never have cell phones. And it's Sunday, so the town supervisor's office is closed."

"Leave that to me," said Bootsie. "I'll find the Binghams at the club today."

"I'll ask Gerda to get on her computer, too!" Sophie added.

At the mention of Gerda, Joe got up and started stuffing his keys, phone, and sunglasses into his pockets.

"I hope Eula wins the lottery and goes on a 'round the world cruise!" said Holly, sitting up and looking uncharacteristically agitated. "One of those cruises that takes, like, two years. Then I wouldn't have to see her in her beige low-heeled pumps anymore! And by the way, just saying the words 'low-heeled pumps' have given me a migraine."

"You know what, there's a Powerball this week," said Joe. "Let's go to the luncheonette and get some tickets and drop them at Eula's house. This could totally get rid of her."

"What if she wins?" Bootsie said. "She might use the money to get more beige outfits. You might end up seeing more of Eula, not less."

"No way," said Holly positively. "Eula was drunk at the club a few months ago, and I overheard her telling the Binghams that her dream is to get on one of those megaboats and see, like, Borneo. "

"Well, I'll throw in five dollars for the Powerball tickets." Bootsie shrugged. "I used to be okay with Eula, but I don't want her stealing all the good stories at the *Gazette*."

"I'm out of here," Joe said. "I'm cleaning out my storage units today, and the cell service is terrible there, so don't try to call me," he said, avoiding Sophie's sad puppy eyes—and her stack of bridal reading material.

As I LEFT Holly's house, I tried to get excited about my new gig at the Pack-N-Ship. At least it was a break from painting, and it would be quiet at the shipping store. It was Sunday, after all, and the front counter was closed for business.

Also, I'd played with all five dogs in the backyard after I fed them breakfast, and vacuumed up a mountain of dog hair from my sofa. I'd take Waffles with me to the Pack-N-Ship, and let John's mixed-breed pack take a group afternoon nap. These dogs were adorable, but I'd started counting down the days till they left.

As Waffles and I drove into town, we passed Le Spa, where Sophie was visible through the front windows, seated in a pedicure chair, reading magazines, with Holly in the next chair. I honked and waved, and Sophie looked up, waving and beckoning me inside.

"Hi, everyone," I said. "And, um, hey Gerda!" I added to her sidekick, who was perched on a nearby stool and didn't look all that happy about being stuck at a beauty parlor.

"Kristin, look who's in this issue of *Food & Wine*!" Sophie handed over the magazine. It was open to a glossy six-page story about the upcoming Fall Restaurant Weekend in Las Vegas, which would feature tons of high-end restaurants and close to twenty thousand guests at the MGM Grand.

"Vegas Restaurant Weekend is sponsored by the Philip LaMonte Restaurant Group, owner of The Lobster Shack, the DooWop Lounge, and seven other Vegas hotspots," she read, pointing to the bottom of the page. "That's Lobster Phil's restaurant empire!"

"Very nice!" I told her. At least Sophie wasn't talking about her Joe problems. "Well, I better head out," I said, feeling a bit sorry for myself. Holly and Sophie both looked totally relaxed with their perfect feet propped up on hot river rocks.

"You know what, for a beauty establishment, which I usually don't like because of frou-frou decor, this is pretty nice place," Gerda said approvingly, looking around Le Spa's Spartan white expanse.

I guess all the white marble and stark walls, plus the blond wood floors, met with her strict Austrian standards for a facility devoted to self-improvement—even if Gerda's more into tight glutes than glowing skin and glossy hair. Not pausing to ask permission, Gerda opened a few random doors, and disappeared for a few minutes into an adjacent room from the spa lounge.

"Miss, there is empty room here to the right," Gerda said, returning to the main room, where Le Spa's owner, Ursula, was massaging Sophie's toes. Gerda gestured to a door she'd opened to a large, square space with a front window and lacquered wood floors. "I see opportunity here."

"We were gonna do waxing in there," said Ursula, who wore her usual sour expression, which was understandable. It can't be easy taking care of Sophie's nail requests, because Sophie gets special manicures tailored to every holiday. "We never got around to it, though."

"I have idea," Gerda said. "I got about twelve hours free every day, even when my boss Barclay, her ex"—here, she pointed at Sophie—"is up for working out. I could do some Pilates classes in there, split profit fifty-fifty with you."

"Huh," said Ursula, looking somewhat askance at the prospect of partnering up with Gerda, but also interested by the mention of profit. "How much do you think you can make?"

"I got a business proposal mostly done, I been looking for the right space to open my own gym," announced Gerda. "Pretty sure with one room and ten clients at forty bucks a pop twice a day, I gonna earn eight hundred bucks every twenty-four hours. So you can get four hundred dollars a day from me." Immodestly, she added, "I'm pretty awesome at what I do, so I'm gonna have clients out the wazoo."

"I'll come, at least a few times a week," promised Holly.

"So you're saying that you can set up this room to bring in, like, two grand a week?" said Ursula, with the biggest smile I'd ever seen on her normally crabby face. "Even if you just do the classes on weekdays?"

"Yup," said Gerda, also wearing one of her infrequent smiles, which, like harvest moons, come around about once a year. "This is gonna be a moneymaker."

"I'm happy for you, Gerda. You deserve your own success," Sophie told her sadly. "I'll come to your classes, if I'm not too brokenhearted by Joe not wanting to marry me."

She sighed tragically, then brightened a little. "Ya know what, I'll pay for your Pilates machines, Gerda. Those things cost a freakin' mint! Ya can't afford them without some help, that's for sure!"

"Thanks," said Gerda, still looking happy. "All I need now is Ursula to tell me how much rent she charge for this room."

"You shouldn't charge her rent, Ursie," Holly told the spa owner. "Everyone who comes in for Pilates will stay to get highlights or a facial. Your business will double by the end of the first week."

"Okay." The stylist shrugged, returning to Sophie's toes armed with a bottle of Chanel Pirate Red polish.

I was astonished. Within the space of five minutes, Gerda had outlined a business plan yielding her eight grand a month, with zero outlay of cash on her part. I was obviously in the wrong line of business.

No wonder I was heading for the Pack-N-Ship—my antiques store was a complete dead end. My boyfriend John had gently suggested I start selling more items on eBay, which I kept meaning to do. I needed to spend less time with my friends, I thought, and more on making money.

"I'm heading to my new job," I said, aiming for a cheery tone. "Bye, everyone!"

I was hoping the group would sense the self-pity underneath my faux-upbeat persona, but everyone was so excited about Gerda's Pilates studio that they barely even said good-bye. Ursula was already up helping Gerda measure for how many reformer machines and yoga mats they could fit into the space, while Holly and Sophie were coming up with a list of moneybags friends they'd invite for the first week of classes.

"Fine," I thought, gunning my Subaru. I might not have any money, but I still had my pride.

Chapter 14

My few shreds of pride vanished quickly when Waffles and I opened the back door to the Pack-N-Ship, using a key Leena had dropped off in my mailbox on Saturday.

I rarely get packages, and since The Striped Awning's eBay sales aren't great, I don't ship them out much, either, and I'd forgotten the Pack-N-Ship's signature scent.

The place was built in the 1950s as a hot dog stand, and the low-slung, shacklike building is undeniably cute, with a front counter where foot-longs were once served, and a back storeroom that once held buns and mustard. Unfortunately, even though the building's been a mail facility for more than twenty years, tit still smells like hot dogs, especially when it rains.

"This will be fun!" I told Waffles as we eyed the dusty, dim storeroom. It looked like a bomb had gone off, which isn't a comforting thought when you're in a mail facility all by yourself.

The place was a complete mess. It looked like Leena hadn't sorted any incoming parcels for the past month, and she seemed pretty far behind on getting packages out the door, too. No wonder packages took so long to get to Bryn Mawr, or leave it. Dozens of boxes were stuffed in the back room where Ball Park franks had once turned on an automated spit.

Leena also can't resist tearing into particularly intriguing-looking packages, then slapping a "Damaged" sticker on the box and taping it back up. Bootsie told me that Leena once admitted after one too many Miller High Lifes that she's always hoping she'll uncover some kind of crazy drug ring operating via her mail store. Apparently, that's how Leena justifies ripping open random boxes. This doesn't affect me often, but Holly and Joe, who are both big online shoppers, are outraged by Leena.

While Waffles sniffed around, I tried to make sense of the various sorting bins and pallets, which Leena had described as "Self-explanatory! Any idiot could do the job!"

It *was* pretty easy work, I thought, as I turned on a tiny radio on Leena's messy desk, feeling pretty sorry for myself as I loaded packages into huge bins on wheels by the loading dock of the tiny building. There was a bin for outgoing packages under a pound, and then a pallet for larger local boxes. The other bins and pallets were for boxes headed to any zip codes south of Delaware or west of Ohio.

The inbound group of unsorted packages was smaller, since only packages that require a signature land at the Pack-N-Ship. Still, though, a ton of boxes headed to residents of our village were tossed pell-mell near Leena's desk. People had to be wondering where the shoes, books, and barbecue sauce they'd ordered were! Two hours later, I had gotten through almost half the chaotic mountain of packages, and my self-pity had reached an all-time high. I mean, who else in town was stuck in a smelly storeroom on a Sunday afternoon?

Well, anyone who worked at the Publix, the hardware store, the Old Navy, and the Lowe's out by the mall probably were, but at least those places didn't smell like old hot dogs. I began to understand why Leena illegally rips into packages: Quite a few boxes were half open. There were gardening tools headed to my next door neighbors Hugh and Jimmy Best, and fishing equipment from Orvis ordered by Chef Skipper. Gerda had a tracksuit shipped to her chez Barclay. The Colketts had a bunch of packages from Ralph Lauren and Bergdorf Men's, which explained how they always looked so impeccable.

I paused when I got to the biggest package I'd seen all day—a three-foot-by-five-foot box about twelve inches in depth, with a 90210 zip code for its destination. It weighed maybe twenty-five pounds, and its size made it awkward to lift. Then I noticed the recipient's address: Viale, on Wilshire Boulevard.

Gianni's swanky new Beverly Hills restaurant!

The box was undeniably painting-shaped, had been received on Thursday, and was more than heavy enough to contain an ornate frame and a Hasley Huntingdon-Mews canvas worth two hundred and fifty thousand dollars!

Had Bootsie actually been right? Maybe Gianni had stolen *Heifer in Tomato Patch*, and was mailing it to himself via UPS Ground.

FOR SEVERAL MINUTES, I gingerly poked at the package, trying to determine what its contents were. Leena had charged $50.75 to ship it, but as usual, she hadn't bothered to get it out the door and onto a westbound truck. I noticed there was no return address, either, and the label had been paid for and printed at home . . . which meant the box could have been dropped off in Leena's mail bin outside the hot dog stand.

Unfortunately, it was one of the few boxes Leena hadn't ripped into, so I called Bootsie.

"THIS IS PERFECT timing, because I just spent thirty minutes drinking pink wine with the Binghams at the club and talking about Maison de Booze," Bootsie told me five minutes later, after she'd arrived via the back entrance and dragged the package over to the loading dock, where she was eyeing it with interest.

"The Binghams said they never heard of Mega Wine Mart—they were contacted by a guy named Barry Tutto, who told them he wanted to buy the old garden store and turn it into Maison de Booze, which sounded so fabulous that they agreed immediately," Bootsie told me. "They never met this guy Barry, but that their lawyer got an agreement of sale from him in the mail, and they happily signed. They think I'm joking about Mega Wine Mart!" she added, annoyed. "I made them promise to get me this Tutto guy's phone number. "Now, let's rip into this package, pronto!" she said, grabbing a box cutter from Leena's messy desk.

"It's a federal offense to open other people's mail," I told her.

"That's mail fraud," she told me confidently. "That's different."

"Tampering with mail is illegal, too! Which I'm pretty sure you're about to do," I told her.

"It's different these days," Bootsie told me with complete assurance. "You don't abide by those ancient rules, do you? People send weird stuff through the mail, and it's gotta be checked by someone."

"Yeah, but we don't think this is something dangerous—we think it's Honey's painting," I reminded Bootsie.

Bootsie dragged the package over to the back door and out onto the loading dock where she could see it better.

"What's more illegal—stealing a pricey painting, or opening a teeny little package?" Bootsie shrugged. "Walt will probably give us an award. Plus, and I really shouldn't have to keep reminding you of this, I'm a *journalist*."

"We should call Walt," I told Bootsie, ignoring her flimsy I'm-a-reporter rationalization, which she falls back on every time she's about to do something illegal or ill-advised. "Maybe he can get a court order, or whatever you need to seize mail."

"You know what?" Bootsie told me. "I just remembered"—here, she gave me a meaningful wink—"that this package was already busted when we got here."

She rifled through Leena's desk and slapped a "Damaged" sticker on the box. With that, she deftly made an incision at the very edge of the top left corner. She gently peeled open the corner flap, revealing layers of brown paper—and then a gilt frame . . .

"I knew it!" screamed Bootsie.

Honestly, I was shocked. It looked like this really *was* Honey's painting. Bootsie was poised to keep ripping, but just then, a blue Ford Festiva bearing the Pack-N-Ship logo on the door rolled into the back parking lot, and Leena hopped out.

"Hey there, ladies!" Leena said cheerily. "Figured you might need a break right about now. Hey, Bootsie's here, too—awesome! I picked up some baked Lay's and onion dip, and I've got an Igloo full of Miller High Life!"

WHILE LEENA FLIPPED open her trunk to grab her cooler-on-wheels, Bootsie dragged the package back up the loading dock, and shoved it into a corner, all at lightning speed. Meanwhile, I quietly hyperventilated and made small talk with Leena.

Leena herself rips open packages, but I doubted she'd be happy with Bootsie doing the same—and especially under my watch, on my first day as mail sorter. I wiped perspiration from my damp forehead, wishing for the millionth time that Bootsie would hurry up and head to the Delaney family lakeside cabin in Maine, like she does each August.

Luckily, Leena didn't notice my mini-panic, and within a few minutes, she'd cranked up the country music in her Festiva, cracked open the beers and chips, and was hosting a mini-party with our legs dangling off the loading dock.

I relaxed a little. Beer is beer, even if you're drinking it outside a hot-dog-scented mail facility. Still, I was supposed to be working till four that afternoon, and it was only 3:35.

"I'm still on the clock, Leena," I told the clerk, who was deep in a conversation with Bootsie about some Orvis hiking boots that Bootsie had ordered and that Leena had just happened to open by mistake and try on. "I'll just keep working till four."

And tape that box back up, I mentally added.

"Naw, you're done for the day! I'll pay you till four," Leena told me with a dismissive wave of a baked Lay's.

"Personally, I mentally check out from work around noon," she added. "By two when the counter closes, all I can think about is a nap and some Kathie Lee and Hoda on my DVR.

"Another beer?" she offered. "No? Bootsie, I know I can count on you!"

Chapter 15

On Monday, the sun was shining, the sky was a brilliant blue, and my mood was jubilant as walked outside and looked at The Striped Awning from a customer's-eye-view.

I felt a surge of hope. I'd finished my second coat of Smashing Pink. The color was incredibly cheerful! I mean, who could resist entering an all-pink store with an adorable basset hound looking out from the front windows? Plus I hadn't been party to mail fraud! And, my boyfriend would be home tomorrow from his vet clinic. Things were definitely on the upswing.

"The pink looks pretty good," said Bootsie, who showed up with Joe at eleven-fifteen.

"I just came from the Pack-N-Ship, where I was going to grab that box and take it to Walt," she told me. "I told Leena I left my phone in the back room, but when I went back there, the package headed to Beverly Hills was gone. I checked every single bin—which you did a nice job organizing, by the way."

"Maybe it shipped out already," I said hopefully. I'd had a chance to quickly tape up the incision Bootsie had made before we finally parted ways with Leena at five-thirty the night before, and positioned the package to go out on the first truck today.

"I've been thinking," I added. "That package could have been a lot of things—maybe a mirror or a painting the Colketts picked out for the place. We don't know it was *Heifer.*"

"Well, thanks to you, we'll never know, because the package was stolen last night," Bootsie informed me. "Leena's regional truck doesn't come until noon, and nothing was sent out yet this morning. Plus Leena admitted she forgot to lock up last night. So, someone grabbed the Viale package."

Bootsie had called Walt to report the incident. Naturally, she'd bent the truth a bit in this conversation, telling Walt that she'd been helping me at the Pack-N-Ship when she happened to notice a damaged box with a gilt frame peeking out. Walt had promised to look into the missing package.

"Now I'm working full time on my Mega Wine Mart story," Bootsie finished. "Something's funky with this franchise. There is no one named Barry Tutto in all of Pennsylvania, New Jersey, or Delaware, at least according to the Internet!"

"Yoo-hoo!" sang out Mrs. Bingham, popping into the shop at that moment. "Kristin, this pink paint is an absolute hoot! So cheerful!"

"Thanks so much," I said, gratified that someone liked it.

"Fun," agreed Mr. Bingham. "Can we take you all over to the club for lunch?"

"Did you find Barry Tutto's number yet?" Bootsie replied rudely, ignoring the lunch invite, which sounded kind of fun to me. "Because you and Barry Tutto are subjecting this town to the biggest and most environmentally unsound megastore for miles. We're talking forty thousand square feet of concrete retail eyesore!"

The Binghams, both in sky-blue polos today and a jaunty pair of cat-eye sunglasses on Mrs. B., stared at Bootsie for a minute, then burst out laughing.

"Bootsie, you are too much!" said Mr. Bingham. "You have to stop with that crazy story about a superstore. It's just going to be a tiny wine shop with free cheese."

"No it isn't!" screamed Bootsie. "There's a huge billboard right over the golf course for the discount wine store. Look up when you get to the club!"

"That's not going to be on our old garden store property," Mrs. Bingham said, waving a hand dismissively. "You're such a prankster! Not that I'd *mind* having discount wine in town."

"Sounds fun," agreed her husband. "Anyway, we looked all over, but Barry's number is nowhere to be found. And I can't ask my lawyer for it, hon," he told Bootsie, anticipating her next question. "Every time I exchange one word with that gal, she charges me five hundred dollars. Well, bye, kids!"

I thought Bootsie's head might explode, but she eventually calmed down and went back to Googling on her iPhone.

"I couldn't find any Barry Tutto, and there's still no info online about the new megastore. It's almost like they're trying to stay under the radar, except for the giant sign. The press release lists an anonymous holding company as the owner of the franchise, and a generic e-mail address, but no phone number or name of a contact person. And I've sent three e-mails since yesterday, with no reply."

"The Town Board of Supervisors is only made up of three people: Mrs. Potts, Jimmy Best, and Officer Walt," said Joe. "Won't that group want to stop a huge wine warehouse from bulldozing a beautiful forest?"

"Any place that serves liquor is pretty much an automatic yes with the Board of Supervisors," explained Bootsie. "Mega Wine Mart got approved a few weeks ago. Mrs. Potts told me that she didn't read the fine print, either, and when she heard about something called Maison de Booze, she voted yes. Anyway, they still gotta get it through zoning—but it's a shoo-in approval, too, because those folks love to drink."

Bootsie dialed Town Zoning, but hung up a minute later. "The whole office is closed this week for a storm water management conference in Scottsdale," she said. "They didn't even leave their receptionist on duty."

Her phone dinged with a text, while Joe eyed my paint job more closely, removing a few of the tarps I'd draped around The Striped Awning.

"Gianni did get back to town on first thing Thursday morning, not on the late-afternoon flight!" Bootsie crowed happily, reading from her phone. "Both the airline and his cameraman confirmed that he took a red-eye from L.A. on Wednesday night and told Randy to lie about it if anyone asked him! Then Gianni disappeared all day on some mysterious errand—which was probably sneaking into the club and grabbing *Heifer*!

"Right now, though," she finished, "I'm making a visit to the headquarters of Mega Wine Mart, and I'll need you to go with me."

"As much fun as that sounds, I'm staying at The Striped Awning," said Joe. "I'm depressed, and this pink paint job isn't helping. Luckily, I just cleaned out my storage units, and I think I can save this place."

Excitement soared within me, since I'd been concerned that my mini-makeover wasn't quite working. Joe is honestly excellent at decorating, and when he's upset, only a project makes him feel better. If he worked his magic on The Striped Awning, it would look amazing!

"Er . . . there's one small detail if I go to Jersey with Bootsie," I said, indicating Waffles, who was lying on his dog bed, staring hopefully at Joe, wagging. And looking totally adorable!

"Fine. He gets one peepee walk and a Milk-Bone. That's it," said Joe, reaching into his tote bag for some fabric swatches.

"Also, there are four dogs at my house that need a bathroom break at three," I told him. "You know where the key is under the flowerpot."

"Will you be done fixing this place up by Wednesday?" Bootsie asked Joe. "Because tomorrow's *Gazette* is running a page three story about the all-new Striped Awning. I've also invited the whole town to a reopening party to unveil your signature cock tail," she told me. "It's Wednesday at 5 p.m. I'll supply the alcohol and Triscuits."

"Thanks!" I said gratefully.

FIFTEEN MINUTES LATER, after a quick stop at the luncheonette where I'd been surprised to see Skipper manning the grill counter, and another detour to pick up Sophie and Gerda, we were back on the Atlantic City Expressway.

While she drove, Bootsie started removing her clothes—at least the outer layer, which was an L.L. Bean tracksuit, which I'd thought was a strange choice for an eighty-one-degree day.

Underneath, she wore a red Pack-N-Ship shirt and a hideous pair of knee-length shorts. The shirt wasn't much better—a boxy button up with short sleeves and "Leena, Store Manager" inscribed above the jaunty Pack-N-Ship logo.

"I'm guessing there's a reason you're wearing a uniform," I sighed.

"Absolutely—big box stores are all about cheap shipping," Bootsie told me through mouthfuls of an egg sandwich on fragrant multigrain toast.

"Did you tell Leena you're going to impersonate her today?" I said.

"I don't think I mentioned it," Bootsie said, finishing half her lunch in four bites. "But she had a bunch of uniforms in the storeroom, so I borrowed one yesterday when you were moving Holly's packages into their own pallet."

"Leena's going to think I took it!" I said, embarrassed.

"She probably won't even notice. Leena isn't real detail-oriented," Bootsie observed.

"Yum!" said Sophie, taking a dainty bite of her sandwich.

"Normally, I don't eat protein and carbs in same meal," Gerda informed us from the backseat, "but today I cannot resist combination of egg and bread."

"Now that Skipper's running the place, the food's never been better," Bootsie told her—which was true. The combination of fluffy eggs, arugula, and a drizzle of olive oil and sea salt on multigrain toast was a huge leap up from the old breakfast specials.

"Skipper's instituted Breakfast All Day à la McDonald's, and the town response has been huge! We're doing a front-page story on it this week," Bootsie said. "Anyway, I ran into the Colketts there when I was getting coffee this morning, and got some info about that lady Nonna Claudia. They told me she hates Gianni! She's got some three-year contract with him, though, so she has to keep working for him, and he pays her out the wazoo."

As Bootsie headed east, she relayed a sad tale spun by the Colketts about how Nonna Claudia had been flown out the month before to work with the Gianni's California staff on pasta, and like the Colketts, she had been living in a swanky hotel suite paid for by the Food Network. But after a week, Nonna had informed Gianni she didn't like L.A.

"She finally convinced Gianni to send her back here from Beverly Hills to finish out the last months of her pasta contract. She's apparently saving money to go back and buy a farmhouse in Sicily. Or something," Bootsie said vaguely.

"Does the luncheonette gig mean Skipper is done with the club forever, even when Gianni goes back to California?" I asked, concerned. There was no way that the tiny diner could ever match Skipper's salary at the country club.

"Right now, the club and Gianni aren't good topics to bring up with Skipper," said Bootsie. "But I think he's looking at this as a temporary job. Anyway, I need you to find out who handles operations for Mega Wine Mart," she told me, handing me her iPhone.

After some quick Googling, I gave her the name—Chad Smith.

"We could kidnap him and beat the crap out of him," suggested Gerda. "Then he tell you whatever you need to know."

"That's a good Plan B," said Bootsie. "Let's back-burner that, and hope Chad likes tall blondes in uniform!"

MEGA WINE MART's corporate headquarters were in Atlantic City, in a new, glass-fronted office building several blocks in from the ocean and the casinos.

The logo included a giant goblet of red wine, a bunch of neon grapes, and the company names in large block letters, and it appeared that the whole three-story building was devoted to the dissemination of tasty discount intoxicants.

"Business must be good," I noted, reluctantly following Bootsie inside the well air-conditioned lobby, where a map was dotted with goblets that marked the location of each Mega Wine Mart from California to Florida.

I'd thought about staying in the car with Sophie, who had a call scheduled with her lawyers, but finally decided to go inside with Bootsie and Gerda. They just didn't seem like a safe pair.

If Bootsie's postal persona didn't work out, I could tell the Mega Wine Mart people Bootsie had recently gone off her meds against the advice of a team of medical experts, and drag her out as quickly as possible.

"I wonder if it's too late to get a piece of the franchise in Bryn Mawr," mused Bootsie, taking note of another wall in the lobby that listed dozens of types of wine, champagne, and Prosecco carried by the chain. "This store's gonna *kill* in our town."

"We're here to *stop* the franchise, remember?" I whispered to her.

"Oh, right. Well, if they go ahead with it, I mean," she said, unperturbed, and walked up to the receptionist, clipboard in hand and toothy grin in place.

"Hi!" she told a bored-looking girl behind a huge beige desk. "I'm Leena McElvoy, and I'm here to see Chad Smith."

"Do you have an appointment?" asked the girl, who didn't look all that excited about her job, or about Bootsie's annoyingly upbeat persona.

"Absolutely," said Bootsie. "We're from Pack-N-Ship Bulk Transport, South Jersey Regional Division, and I e-mailed him last week."

"Your shirt says 'Store Manager,'" pointed out the receptionist. "How come it says 'Store Manager' if you're from Regional?"

"I got promoted," said Bootsie. "And here's some free advice: Maybe if you put a smile on that puss, you'd get a better job, too."

The receptionist, who was about 23 years old with a blond ponytail, stared Bootsie down for a long minute.

"My job might suck, but at least I'm not wearing a hideous red Pack-N-Ship shirt and unflattering Bermuda shorts," the blonde said. "Bam!" she added, then dialed Chad, who appeared a moment later, a pleasant if confused smile on his face. He was somewhere in his late thirties, without much of a tan for a guy who lived at the Jersey shore, and was decked out in a Caesar's polo shirt and black pants.

"Chad! Hi!" said Bootsie, handing him one of Skipper's sandwiches. "Remember, I e-mailed about bringing you some lunch and talking our great new rates for high-volume ground shipping!"

"Uh, gosh, I'm not sure," said the guy. "But come on back to my office, I guess."

"Sorry I didn't bring you anything," Bootsie told the receptionist with a fake smile. "You probably don't like avocado and Manchego with tarragon vinaigrette on a baguette anyway."

"Uh-huh," said the girl. "Maybe if you cut down on the baguettes, you'd look better in those shorts."

"Soooo, bulk shipping, great." Chad nodded, sitting at a new-looking desk in an office with an accent wall the color of cabernet and a view of the parking lot, where I could see Sophie getting worked up on her phone call. Chad unwrapped the sandwich, and dug in.

"You like to hang out at Caesar's?" Bootsie asked.

"I deal Texas Hold 'Em in the VIP Poker Lounge three nights a week," he said through a mouthful of cheese and veggies. "Dealing poker's how I bought my condo and my Porsche. I mean, I love wine and this is a cool day job, but Caesar's is where I really make bank."

"I love Caesar's!" Bootsie told him, while I wondered if this was true. The Delaney/McElvoy clan does have a gambling streak, and Bootsie and her mom make occasional road trips to the casinos, so I guess they might frequent the place.

Chad looked flattered, and I noticed him checking out Bootsie's tanned tennis-honed legs. It's funny with Bootsie—she doesn't get the constant ogling that Holly and Sophie receive, but there's a certain type of guy that loves Bootsie's tomboy sporty quality. As luck would have it, Chad appeared to like what he saw.

"Anyway, Chad, we understand you guys are opening a new store outside Philly, and that falls in my region."

"That's true, but we have a great deal with FedEx Ground," Chad told her. "I'd love to help you out, but I don't see you being able to undercut FedEx. And Corporate doesn't run daily operations at the franchises. You'd need to talk to the individual store's owners."

"I know!" said Bootsie. "And I was all set to do that, until this one"—here, she poked an elbow in my direction—"lost the paperwork we had for the new store! She left it in a cab after getting super-drunk at the Borgata last week."

I assumed an expression of boozy regret, while Chad looked confused again and kept working his way through his sandwich.

"Who's this?" asked a tough-looking lady in a dark suit, poking her head and staring suspiciously at me, Bootsie, and Gerda. "Are you from Pack-N-Ship?" she said, eyeing Bootsie's shirt logo. "Because Chad isn't authorized to make any changes in shipping."

"No problem!" said Bootsie, jumping up and thankfully looking ready to go. "We just added some new bulk shipping rates I wanted to make you aware of. Well, we gotta go talk to the purchasing agent at Harrah's."

"You do that," said the woman, giving Bootsie a nasty look. "Meeting in two minutes, Chad, in the boardroom." She took off down the hall.

Bootsie then went spectacularly off-script. "Chad, I'm gonna tell you the truth. Shipping isn't what we're after here. We're actually from Bryn Mawr, and want the Wine Mart franchise for ourselves!" she whispered.

"Apparently some guy named Barry Tutto is behind the new location, and we need to get hold of him. If you can just give us a copy of the paperwork for the franchise outside Philly, that would be awesome," she finished. "We want to undercut Tutto and open the store in Bryn Mawr ourselves. And of course we'd want you to come to the opening, and we'll host you for a blowout dinner afterward!"

Chad followed us out. "I can't give you the file here," he whispered once we were out of earshot of the sour-faced receptionist. "I mean, I'd love to see you in on the franchise, but I'm gonna need to do the handoff later during my shift at Caesar's and I get a dinner break around seven-forty-five. Here's my number. Text me when you get there!"

THIRTY MINUTES LATER, Sophie led us into a BCBG store at the Atlantic City outlet mall.

"You can't go to a casino in a tracksuit or shorts," she told Bootsie and Gerda, which, based on my limited knowledge of casinos, isn't strictly true.

"Kristin is barely squeaking by with that sundress," Sophie added. "No offense, but I think I saw that one on the clearance rack at Target last week when I was buying a twelve-pack of toilet paper!"

"You did," I told her. "That's where I got it."

"Let me grab a few things for you two to try on," Sophie told Bootsie, who shrugged, and Gerda, who looked annoyed.

"These dresses not for me," Gerda told her, casting a doubtful eye at the low-cut outfits all around us. "I don't do sexy."

"You'd look super cute in a jumpsuit!" shrieked Sophie, heading for a rack of zip-up garments.

"I don't do cute," said Gerda.

Meanwhile, I was wondering about Barclay. He was supposedly in Atlantic City, wasn't he? What if he was at Caesar's for dinner or something when we went to meet Chad? It's not like Bootsie and Gerda, who are both six feet tall, are inconspicuous. And while I've never actually met Barclay, since he was unconscious the first time I encountered him, I'm petrified of him.

"Gerda!" I hissed as she shook her head no at every outfit Sophie took off the racks. "What if we run into Barclay? Won't he be mad if you're not, like, home mowing his lawn or something?"

"I install Find My Friends app on his phone a couple months ago," Gerda said, with evident satisfaction. "I been checking on him all week. He never leave the Borgata, which isn't good 'cause they got a lot of great places to eat there, and Barclay can't resist anything by Wolfgang Puck."

After some arguing and negotiating, Bootsie decided she was going all-in, and grabbed the brightest, slinkiest numbers she could find. Forty seconds later, she popped out of the dressing room in an orange bandage dress and strappy heels.

"You look awesome in that!" said a girl with incredibly long black hair to Bootsie. The girl had just emerged from another curtained-off cubicle in a strapless dress made from scuba material.

Bootsie did look downright fantastic, since all that tennis has left her with seriously toned thighs—picture the fat-free legs of the U.S. Women's Soccer Team, and you get the idea.

"Thanks!" said Bootsie, admiring herself in a full-length mirror. "It's a family trait. All the women in the Delaney family have a great ass."

"Where are you girls hanging out tonight?" the girl asked Bootsie and Sophie, encompassing our whole group in the question, including Gerda, who was still behind a closed curtain with her jumpsuits. "I see you work at Pack-N-Ship from that uniform you had on. You must really need a drink bad if you work there!"

"You know it," Bootsie told her, yanking on the hem of her dress. "Especially because this one"—here, she pointed at me—"works there, too, and she's, like, weeks behind on sorting packages!"

"You should come with me and my friends to Savage Men After Dark! We got a VIP booth for my friend's birthday for the seven o'clock show, and if you kick in thirty dollars each, you'll get a free drink and a guaranteed table visit from the dancers!"

"What's Savage Men After Dark?" I asked, mental alarm bells going off, but Bootsie and Sophie were already peeling twenties out of their wallets.

The girl, who told us her name was Mindy, explained she'd gotten ten half-price tickets from a friend at Caesar's, and it was going to be super-fun. She handed over the tickets and drink vouchers as Gerda grimly emerged from her curtained cubicle in a black sleeveless jumpsuit, and balked at changing her sneakers for the leopard pumps that Sophie had selected for her.

"Sneakers are okay for casinos," Gerda said, as we gazed down at the tickets from Mindy, which were emblazoned with black and white photos that confirmed my worst fears. Savage Men was just what it sounded like: shirtless guys in tear-away tracksuits and trench coats. "Come on, Gerda!" shrieked Sophie. "The jumpsuit and heels are on me."

Two hours later, Bootsie, Sophie, Mindy, and her friends were on their third drink while I sipped a single glass of wine, waiting desperately for Chad the poker dealer's text on Bootsie's phone, which I'd stuck right in front of me on the table. Gerda was only drinking seltzer, but seemed to be enjoying the spectacle before us.

Bootsie's attention issues had kicked in big-time thanks to the flashing strobe lights and muscled-up guys on stage, so I kept one eye on the screen and the other on the muscles and spray tans. Finally, a text popped up at seven-forty-five.

"Chad says he'll be in the Toga Bar in five minutes," I told Bootsie, who thankfully threw her last handful of dollar bills at a guy onstage who'd just torn off his pants.

"We gotta go," she told Mindy, and exchanged group hugs with the other three girls at the table, along with phone numbers and promises to get together again soon.

At the Toga Bar, Chad was in a booth with a mojito in hand.

"This never happened!" he told us as he handed over the file, with a tipsy edge in his voice that had me worried about his ability to deal out six more hours of Texas Hold 'Em. Was he permitted to drink at work?

"By the way, you look great in that dress!" he added to Bootsie, who was buying Chad another cocktail when Sophie gave a happy little scream.

"Lobster Phil!" shrieked Sophie. "Look, he's sitting right there waving to us. It's another sign!"

Chapter 16

PHIL WAS ENJOYING his namesake dish, grilled and topped with butter and crabmeat, at a swanky eatery just off the gaming floor, and he gallantly rose and invited us all to sit down.

"I go to ladies' room," said Gerda, heading off into the crowded lobby.

"You girls hungry?" he asked. "I'll order a few more lobsters."

Bootsie was about to enthusiastically agree when my phone rang.

"How many dogs are there supposed to be at your house?" Joe said dispiritedly. "I opened the door, and it was like one hundred dogs busted free. They're all over your yard, barking and running."

"There are four!" I told him. "Four dogs, plus Waffles, which is five! You didn't leave Waffles at the store, did you?"

"No, I brought him back to your house," Joe told me, sounding aggrieved. "He's here somewhere. By the way, he drooled all over my custom Valcona leather interior, and I'm not sure my Audi will ever be the same again."

"We need to go, but thanks for offering to buy us dinner," I told Phil.

"Is that my Honey Bunny?" said Sophie, forgetting she was mad at Joe.

"Okay," I heard Joe mumble. "I count five dogs. They're all back in the house now. I'm throwing down some kibble and running out the door." I hung up.

"Too bad you're leaving," said Phil. "I just got done a bunch of meetings over at the Borgata. What brings you ladies to A.C., anyway?"

Sophie explained that we'd driven over from Pennsylvania because a new wine store was opening, and it was real upsetting for people who wanted to save the forest currently located where the huge store was going to be built. But, she added, a lot of people were super-excited about free wine and cheese nights to be held there on Thursdays and Saturdays.

Lobster Phil sat up straighter. "What's this place called?"

"It was supposed to be a real tiny shop called Maison de Booze, but it turns out it's a Mega Wine Mart," Sophie said.

"I'm intrigued," said Phil, leaning back and folding up his napkin. "You know what, Sophie, I think I *am* gonna come check out this cute town you live in. I'll drive over tomorrow, and you can show me the site for the Mega Wine store."

"Sure!" she said. "I'd love to show ya around. You can check out Gianni's fancy restaurant, too."

"I wouldn't miss it," said Phil thoughtfully, drumming his fingers on the table and beckoning a waiter to remove his plate. "You gals ever hear any more about the painting that got stolen from your friend?"

"I'm eighty-seven percent sure it was stolen by Chef Gianni Brunello, who then dropped it at a Pack-N-Ship store to be mailed to his new restaurant in L.A.," Bootsie told him.

"Gianni might have stolen it?" Phil said, interested. "You can't put anything past that guy. Always was up to no good, even when the two of us had our restaurants in our Jersey days."

Just then, Gerda returned, and I jumped up to leave.

"Sophie, I hate you right now for this jumpsuit," she announced. "You ever try to go to bathroom in one of these?"

SINCE NO ONE else except Gerda was sober, and she doesn't have a license, I steered Bootsie's Range Rover toward Bryn Mawr on the Atlantic City Expressway. Bootsie examined the file from Chad, which wasn't easy in the dim reading light in the passenger seat, while Gerda and Sophie complained being squashed in the back between all the L.L. Bean goods still stuffed into the SUV.

Bootsie tipsily leafed through the half-inch-thick Mega Wine Mart file on the upcoming Bryn Mawr franchise.

"The owners have to be named in here somewhere," she said. "Articles of Incorporation; Brand Continuity; Approved Suppliers—the reading light in this car sucks, I can barely see anything—Fees and Royalties . . . here's something. There's a BT Development listed, but there's no contact info for him other than a law firm in Miami. There's nothing in here about who this Tutto guy is!"

Her phone rang, and she Bluetoothed the call into the car's fancy sound system.

"Did you find out anything about the Mega Wine Mart?" Holly asked.

"We struck out," admitted Bootsie.

"Uh-huh," said Holly, not sounding all that surprised. "Anyway, I've almost recovered from my three months of dealing with Eula, so I need a project, plus thanks to Kristin, I finally received seventeen boxes of clothes and shoes that she found in the back room at the Pack-N-Ship."

"Ooh, I want to come see what ya got!" said Sophie.

"Anyhoo, I can't stop wondering if Honey's painting was in that box you saw yesterday headed to California," Holly said, a slightly manic edge in her voice that I know all too well and usually precedes either shopping or Internet stalking to make sure her husband isn't cheating.

Once a year or so, Holly bands together with Bootsie and Gerda on one of their investigative boondoggles. Sometimes this trio gets results, or they find themselves being faced down by an angry wife who shows up, screams at them, and drags her husband away—which happened last winter at a lounge called Tiki Joe's in Florida.

"So I'm heading over to Gianni's restaurant right now to get him liquored up and find out if he knows about the box," Holly told us.

"Count me in!" said Sophie. "Joe's text mentioned an all-nighter at Kristin's store, which he said is, like, a fiasco, decor-wise."

"I go, too, to Gianni's," announced Gerda. "Gianni a real hands-y guy. No girl safe with him."

"Um, I have five dogs at my house, so I probably shouldn't come," I told the group, desperate for the day to end. "You've got this plan under control," I added encouragingly.

"Gerda and I will swing by your house and pick ya up after you feed all those dogs!" said Sophie.

"You guys don't need me for this!" I told Sophie. "Holly and Gerda have a special technique for information gathering. They're like a dream team!"

Sophie's huge brown eyes welled up with tears.

"I need my friends around me." She sniffed. "I'm in crisis. If Joe won't even look at the *Town & Country* jewelry ads, how are we going to get engaged? Plus my ex is trying to take my new house and all my shoes. And I hate being alone. I get real depressed!"

"Okay," I agreed hastily. "We're almost back at The Striped Awning. Everyone can get their own cars and then you and Gerda can pick me up in twenty minutes at my house. But I refuse to stay later than eleven at Gianni's!"

"I'll get what I need from him by ten-forty-five," said Holly, and hung up.

Chapter 17

"COME HERE, YOU sexy girl!" Gianni told Holly when we got to his restaurant. The chef hopped over on his crutches to nail Holly with a double cheek kiss, then aimed for her lips, which she neatly averted with a merry little laugh and hair toss.

"I got the vodka ready for you!" Gianni told Holly. "Or champagne. Whatever you want!" Just then, he noticed the rest of us trooping in behind her.

"And for your friends, too, I guess," he said, looking none too happy about it as he poured us all drinks from the festive pitcher of cocktails he'd stirred up. The restaurant's tables were empty of diners, and a lone busboy was draping them with crisp white linens for the next day.

The kitchen was gleaming, but no cooks remained, and it looked like the dishwashers were about to leave for the night, which wasn't surprising given that it was a Monday.

"I don't drink alcohol," Gerda informed him. "Although I just been to Atlantic City, and I tempted. For now, I take sparkling water, no ice."

As Gianni grumpily soda-gunned a seltzer, I thought to myself that Holly must have ordered some really great clothes over the past few months, because the dress she wore was absolutely gorgeous.

It was an indigo strapless number with built-in corseting and a subtle slit in the knee-length skirt. Like me, Holly doesn't have cleavage, but the structure of this amazing dress gave her something close to it.

"That's the Jason Wunumber I saw at the mall!" whispered Sophie, nodding to the amazing dress. "And Holly busted out the Sergio Rossi cage sandals, too. No man can resist those!"

"Holly, this great timing, I was gonna call you tonight and invite you to a special top-secret party tomorrow night," Gianni went on. "Gianni about to get even more rich and famous with a new business venture!"

"Are ya opening another restaurant, Chef?" asked Sophie, after succumbing to the same smooch-filled greeting as Holly.

"Even better!" he told her. "What I gonna announce tomorrow will be trendsetter! You all invited," he told us. "Be here at restaurant at 6 p.m.

"Hey, Sophie, why don't I sit between you and Holly here at the bar? I could be, like, a Gianni sandwich between you two gorgeous blondes!"

Gerda cracked her knuckles at this statement, while Holly gave an eye roll, but managed to keep smiling in Gianni's direction.

"I don't want to mess up my new jumpsuit," Gerda told Gianni, "but you being real inappropriate, and I can punch you in face if I need to."

"I need pasta," Bootsie announced to Gianni, plopping herself down next to Holly, as Gerda loomed ominously behind her. "I'm super hungry. Can you whip up that wild mushroom and pro-sciutto dish you do with the agnolotti?"

"Kitchen is closed. But I can call Nonna Claudia down," Gianni offered. "She could do you a pasta."

"You know what, Gianni," Holly told him, "I've been thinking of eating carbs again—at least on holidays and alternate weekends."

She jumped up and out of reach of the chef's roving hands. "Let's go make pasta together, and who knows, maybe next summer, I'll throw a dinner party on the holistic meditation terrace the Colketts are going to design for me," she added.

With this, Holly indicated the restaurant's open kitchen, which was gleaming with its stainless steel just past the bar. "You can give me a quick cooking lesson!" she added.

"This could be pretty sexy," Gianni agreed, jumping up as fast as his crutches would let him. "You ever see that movie *Ghost* when the couple making some kind of pottery thing together? This pasta gonna be like that for us!"

"Absolutely," agreed Holly serenely, then turned to give Gerda desperate raised eyebrows and hand signals indicating that she needed her to burst into the kitchen sometime within the next seven minutes.

"Gianni needs the music!" shouted the chef, ripping off his white chef's jacket to showcase his tattoos in a white T-shirt. "We gonna blast Pitbull!" Catchy Latin pop was soon blasting into the bar and kitchen.

"By the way, Gerda," Bootsie said, sipping her drink, "are you good at tennis?"

"I'm excellent at all sports," Gerda informed her.

"Great, because Mummy has a sore ankle, and I need a new doubles partner tomorrow. You free at two?"

"Absolutely," said Gerda, cracking her knuckles. "Tennis very big in Austria."

All we could see past the bar were Gianni's limbs, which were moving like arms on a slot machine—up, down and all around Holly's slender waist and shoulders. How the man could simultaneously toss dough, sauté wild mushrooms, and grope was quite a feat, especially since he was down to one leg.

"I go into kitchen to supervise," said Gerda finally. "This guy creeping me out."

"How's that pasta coming?" asked Bootsie, shouting across the bar and over a catchy Pitbull tune.

"I was just asking the chef what kind of art he likes," Holly told us through the open kitchen window, "and whether he's buying any paintings for his new place in Beverly Hills, but he told me he doesn't care about stuff like that and leaves it to the Colketts."

"Are ya sure, Chef?" Sophie said. "What about, like, paintings with cows in them? Cows are real relaxing to look at."

"Animals not for Gianni's walls," Gianni told her. "They for the plate, after they're cured, grilled or roasted. Anyway, I don't care about art. Gianni focus on the food."

He expertly sliced at a whopping piece of pork, producing slices so thin you could see through them, and fired up olive oil, shallots, and herbs in a pan—which smelled incredible.

"So you haven't been, um, acquiring any fabulous paintings at all and shipping them out to your new place?" confirmed Holly.

"I got more important stuff than that to do!" Gianni said, downing his drink and the olives floating in it.

"Now we gonna add the prosciutto to the sauté pan, and the ripe little tomatoes—reminds me of your skinny but sexy self!" he told Holly. His hand moved toward Holly's tomatoes, and he went in for the grab.

"I take care of this," said Gerda. She jumped from her bar stool in a dead run, briefly pausing to flip open the hinged door that led to the back area of the bar and the kitchen, but her spiky size 9 heel got caught in the perforated nonslip floor mats. Blond braids flying, Gerda was aloft for a few hair-raising seconds, then crashed onto Gianni, who'd been staring openmouthed as she sailed toward him.

"*Verdammt!*" she screamed. "These shoes gonna kill me!"

"*Merda!*" erupted the chef, who was facedown on the kitchen tiles, Gerda on top of him. Luckily for Gerda, the chef had cushioned her impact. Unfortunately, though, Gianni himself had been in a compromising position at the moment he landed.

"You make me land on prosciutto knife!" he screamed at the Pilates pro. "I got razor-sharp blade stuck in my thigh! Gianni in agony--again!"

"Sorry." Gerda shrugged. "Anyway, what we're trying to find out is, did you steal Honey Potts's painting and mail it to yourself at California restaurant?"

"No, you *putana* broad!" he told her, still facedown. "I don't steal nothing. Gianni need medical attention and maybe gonna sue you!"

"Your floor mats are unsafe," said Gerda blithely. "Maybe I sue *you.*"

"I'll just call nine-one-one," announced Holly. "Oooh, it looks like it's the same leg as the injury from Thursday. Poor you."

"Anyway, the pasta looks like it's ready," observed Bootsie, who took over kitchen duties, draining the agnolotti and adding the pillowy pasta to the delicious sauce. She gave it all a toss, and grabbed some take-out containers from a nearby shelf. "We can take this to go."

AFTER THE EMTs came, I went home and jumped into bed with the five dogs. Unfortunately, since I smelled like prosciutto and the dogs spent from midnight till 2 a.m. sniffing my hair and licking my wrists, it wasn't a restful night.

And just because John had only texted me twice during the time he'd been away didn't mean that our relationship was off track—did it? And the fact that I'd thought about Mike Woodford seven times in the past two days didn't mean anything—probably. At least John was due back tomorrow from his vet clinic, I thought happily as I dropped off to sleep at 2 a.m.

Chapter 18

My MOOD SOARED when I opened my eyes at seven on Tuesday morning, even though my bedroom was still full of dogs. Bootsie had promised to be guest counselor at her sons' day camp, which would keep her busy for the morning.

Even more exciting, I'd soon be down to one dog again. John's mutts could vacate my place today and return to his rented condo, relieving me from daily vacuuming and being trampled every time I opened the door.

And The Striped Awning was ready for its big reveal!

Joe's one-day makeover promised to be amazing, at least according to Joe. I'd finally turned off my phone at 2 a.m., since texts had been arriving every fifteen minutes informing me with his usual lack of modesty that with a single can of dark brown paint, some '70s-modern light fixtures, and a vintage 1920s dining room set, he'd taken The Striped Awning from blah to awe.

"And I do *not* want to see Eula's tomato artwork anywhere in that store," he'd told me in his final message of the night. He'd stashed the canvases behind the mop and vacuum cleaner in my back room, and recommended that I tip the town trash guys ten bucks to dispose of them on Monday.

I figured I'd hang them in the shop as soon as Joe went back to Florida next week. The truth is that most of my customers would love Eula's botanical artwork, while only Holly and the Colketts would appreciate his supercool Halston–meets–Hollywood Hills makeover of the shop, even though I couldn't wait to get over there and see it for myself.

I unscrambled myself from my duvet, jumped over several dogs, turned off my ancient window unit air conditioner, and threw open the windows as I fired up the coffee machine. I unleashed the pack into the backyard, jumped in the shower, put my hair in a ponytail, and threw on a black Gap sundress. Given the fact that I'd spent most of the past week on the highways of South Jersey, the yard wasn't looking great, so I headed out front to water the ancient rosebushes and spritz the old flowerpots I'd painted black and filled with pink geraniums.

Across the street at Sanderson, cows wandered around in the sunshine, tails swishing, which brought Mike Woodford to mind—a vision I quickly shut down.

As I aimed a hose toward the roses, I noticed movement just behind the gorgeous hydrangeas in full bloom that lined the front of the estate, including the one beneath which I'd discovered the unconscious form of Barclay Shields the previous spring.

Just beyond the fence was a short girl in a beige outfit, and she was pushing a small but fully loaded wheelbarrow, its contents hidden by a tarp.

Eula.

What was she schlepping across the grounds of Sanderson at seven-forty-five in the morning? Her Miata was parked on Camellia Lane bordering the estate, and I watched her look around furtively, then open the trunk of her Miata, dump whatever was in the wheelbarrow inside, and shove the small single-wheeled cart inside a thick hedge of holly bushes. With that, she roared away in her snazzy little car.

I waited five minutes, then went across the street, nervously parting the hollies to inspect said wheelbarrow. I'd imagined all kinds of horrible possibilities, but the wheelbarrow was empty. I sniffed. It smelled a little funky, but Sanderson itself has a pleasantly farm-y scent that wafts around its hundreds of acres and mingles with the roses and lilies.

There was some old dirt in the wheelbarrow, but nothing along the lines of remains of a human sacrifice.

Was Eula stealing something else from Honey Potts—maybe another family heirloom, something heavy enough that she needed a wheelbarrow? Had she taken Honey's painting, and was now back for the silver candelabra or a marble bust of an ancient Potts patriarch?

I was too scared of Mrs. Potts to ask her if she'd noticed a short girl in beige robbing her house that morning, so I knocked on a different door at Sanderson.

"MIKE, DID YOU just see Eula Morris pushing a wheelbarrow across the cow pasture?" I said, as he greeted me on the front porch of his cute stone cottage near the cow barns. I then grabbed a column to steady myself. Mike was in jeans . . . and nothing else.

I'd never seen him sans shirt before, and between the tan, the pecs, and the smell of Irish Spring soap, it was a lot to take in.

"Come on in," he said. "Hey, Waffles!" The dog ran inside ecstatically, which annoyed me. He absolutely loves Mike, which I feel is misplaced, since Mike isn't boyfriend material.

As I followed Mike into his kitchen, where he thankfully put on a T-shirt, I had a sudden horrible thought.

Had Eula *spent the night* at Mike's?

Was she sneaking off the property so Honey wouldn't see her leaving? Although who does a walk of shame pushing a wheelbarrow?

"Are you and Eula, er, friends?" I asked Mike, who handed me a coffee. "Close friends?" I added.

"We're acquaintances," he told me, popping an English muffin into his toaster. "To answer your other question, I didn't see her this morning, but I'm pretty sure I know what she was doing with the wheelbarrow."

"Mikey?" yelled Honey Potts outside his open window. "You got company?"

Mrs. Potts was the last person I wanted to see! What if Honey thought *I* had stayed over with Mike? She makes me nervous as it is. I needed to leave.

"Bye!" I said, racing out of his house with Waffles in tow and Mike following behind us.

I said a polite but brief hello to Mrs. Potts as I raced up her driveway, while she aimed a suspicious look at me, obviously wondering if I'd just had a racy fling with her hot nephew.

I get the feeling I'm not Mrs. Potts's favorite person ever since Lilly's mom, Mariellen Merriwether, tried to kill me and my neighbors. Mariellen is Mrs. Potts's BFF, and there might be some lingering resentment over the whole episode.

"I'll tell you what Eula had in the wheelbarrow later," Mike called after me. "Over a drink."

FIVE MINUTES LATER I flicked on the lights at The Striped Awning, and blinked at the spectacular scene before me.

My paint tarps were gone, and the shop had been arranged in chic, symmetrical style, with the large round 1970s table Joe had trucked from one of his storage units anchoring the front of the store. The ceiling and moldings were now glossy deep brown, so dark they were almost black, in a chic punctuation to my Smashing Pink walls. He'd added a huge sisal rug and a Sputnik-style glass-and-bronze light fixture, which looked amazing above the round table. The rear area of the shop had been arranged as a lounge-y seating area, with the French settee and dining chairs I'd had in stock and under tarps now creating an inviting vibe. More of Joe's clients' castoffs—cool ikat pillows, Foo dogs, modern little lamps—added a modern touch to the seating area, above which a half-dozen chandeliers I'd bought at flea markets now cast a cozy glow.

I called Joe and rattled on for several minutes about how much I loved what he'd done, and how I'd pay him back one day for all the cool accents he'd installed, and how his storage units deserved their own blog and Instagram account, which he seemed to enjoy. Finally, though, he cut me off.

"It's true—your junk store is suddenly as cool as one of those boutique New York hotels where Bowery meets Boho chic," he agreed. "It's like One Kings Lane exploded in there. I've outdone myself! Anyway, while I was hiding those hideous paintings by Eula in your back room, I had a genius idea to figure out whether Eula took *Heifer*.

"I can't explain right now," Joe added. "I'm heading to my storage units in Holly's SUV, with her as designated driver. I plan to combine tranquilizers, Excedrin Migraine, and alcohol today, so I probably shouldn't take the wheel."

"Maybe you should hold off on the prescription medications," I suggested.

"Anyway," he said, "I'm going to need Bootsie to help me pull off my plan. She needs to make herself available from three till five this afternoon."

"I don't think that will be a problem," I told him. "By the way, I saw Eula sneaking something out of Sanderson today with a wheelbarrow, and I asked Mike Woodford about it, and he said he'll explain later."

"Whatever," said Joe. "I can only focus on one Eula problem at a time."

I was about to hang up when Joe told me that I needed to touch up my paint job on the back wall of the store.

"It needs to be *perfect*," he informed me. "I left a tarp draped over the floor there for you. I lent my peerless talent for design, and you can lend your mediocre skills as painter."

Next, I texted Bootsie that Joe needed her for a special Eula project this afternoon, and would she be done volunteering at her kids' camp by then? She immediately called back, and when I picked up, I could hear children screaming, playing, crying, and shouting in the background.

"Pipe down, kids," she announced. "Go play by the lake."

"Shouldn't you be keeping your attention on the three-year-olds?" I asked, alarmed.

"I'm leaving," she said. "I did an hour of tennis drills with thirty-five toddlers, and I need to conserve my strength to kick Eula's tail this afternoon in the club doubles tourney. The match is at two, then I'll be free to help Joe.

"And get this," she added. "It's me and Gerda versus Eula and Lilly Merriwether!"

"Stomp them! Beat Lilly's skinny ass into the ground!" I found myself shouting. "I mean, I hope you win."

"Oh, we're *going* to win," Bootsie assured me. "Listen, don't forget, Gianni invited us to some top-secret event tonight for his new business. And don't even try to weasel out of coming along!"

I'd actually been planning to do just that, but figured I'd say nothing for now.

"I'm stopping by your shop to see Joe's makeover, but first I need to drop in at the *Gazette* to pitch my story about Gianni's new venture. See you in fifteen," Bootsie told me, and disconnected.

TEN MINUTES LATER, Sophie showed up at the store.

"Wow! This looks real cute," she said, sitting down in the cool new seating area in back. "I can tell Joe did one of his minimakeovers here." Her eyes welled up with tears briefly. "He's soooo good at what he does."

Just then, Bootsie stuck her head inside the door. "Eula stole my Gianni story!" she screamed. "That bitch got to the *Gazette* at eight this morning and grabbed the assignment." She left, vowing revenge.

"I keep thinking about Diana-Maria, Lobster Phil's ex," I told Sophie after Bootsie's exit, hoping to distract my friend from her Joe woes. "Maybe we can look her up on Facebook, or call one of your old friends to ask if she's okay?"

"I found her on Facebook last night while I was posting all the feelings I'm having about me and Joe," Sophie said. "Diana-Maria hasn't been on Facebook for, like, six months! It's kinda weird. She used to put pics up all the time. I knew what she ate for breakfast, lunch, and dinner, like, every freakin' day."

"That doesn't sound good," I said, worried. "Where did she work? Maybe we can try to call her there."

"Diana-Maria had a job selling gorgeous jewelry in the boutique at the Borgata," Sophie told me, and burst into tears. "She handled mega-carat rocks that any girl, especially one from Jersey, would love to get as engagement bling. They keep it in a special counter for high rollers in the back, and it's open 24/7. Picture Mariah Carey's jewelry box, and you get the picture."

It looked like Sophie was again about to start obsessing about when Joe and engagement rings, so I changed the subject.

"How's your lawyer doing with Barclay's legal filing about your new house and the shoes?" I asked her, Windexing the front windows.

"It's all BS!" Sophie yelped. "We got the house petition dismissed already. I bought that place with my own money. I had a lot saved up from when I worked in the cement business, plus sometimes Barclay used to give me cash for my birthday, so that's not community property."

"Uh-huh." I nodded, half listening. Maybe I should buy some extra cheddar and Triscuits for the party tomorrow, I thought, since Bootsie seemed way more focused on the booze than the food. One we got this reopening party done, I'd probably have tons of new customers who'll love the hot-pink walls! And if I didn't, I'd focus on my eBay sales, and if all else failed, I could probably get more hours at the Pack-N-Ship.

"The judge seemed way more interested in the shoes," Sophie told me. "He said he needs to get a deposition from Barclay about my size five and a halfs, but of course, my ex is off in Atlantic City and not returning calls. So the shoes are in limbo."

I nodded sympathetically, concurrently dreaming of a quiet, tranquil existence, weeding my yard and catching up on all my overdue bills. I'd ask Leena if she could give me another few hours a week as package sorter—maybe if I worked on, say, Wednesday nights after I closed the shop, her back room wouldn't be so stuffed with unsent and undistributed boxes every weekend.

"By the way, I just saw the Binghams at the luncheonette," Sophie told me. "They were acting real strange, even for them. They were getting takeout and normally they're so chatty and friendly, but they just waved and left real fast with a bunch of takeout food."

I nodded, thinking maybe Bootsie could go track the Binghams down at their house, which is just a few hundred yards from the club. It was so unlike them to not be out and about, and they always had time to stop for a quick gossip. Maybe one of them hadn't been feeling well?

Or maybe they didn't want to admit they'd knowingly sold the charming old garden shop to Mega Wine Mart—if they'd known about Maison de Booze being a teardown, that is! I was about to grab my phone to call Bootsie when Sophie piped up, "Oh yeah, and I saw your boyfriend at the luncheonette, too!"

"You did?" I asked, pausing, surprised that John was home this early. I hadn't heard from him since early yesterday, when he'd mentioned in a text that he was trying to skip his last meeting and make the drive home later in the day. I'd assumed he'd stayed in West Virginia last night after all, and was en route this morning.

"He said he got back yesterday afternoon and jumped into a doubles match at the club," Sophie said. "And he's gonna be playing today, too, 'cause he and that chiropractor he plays with won! He advanced in the tournament."

She noticed my shocked look, and aimed a concerned gaze at me.

"What—he didn't tell you he got back last night?"

"No, and I have, like, a hundred dogs at my house belonging to him that he could have at least picked up," I said.

"He did say his match ran real late last night and he played under the lights!" Sophie said, trying to make me feel better, and failing.

"And then he said a bunch of the players stayed late for drinks at the club, because there were a bunch of preliminary men's and women's doubles matches yesterday. It turned into a party. It probably got too late to call you!"

"He could have texted me," I whined miserably.

Unless he'd been spending time with his flawless ex, Lilly, last night?

This possibility left me slightly short of breath. John and Lilly had ended their marriage on good terms, and she probably had called to let him know she was in town.

Why *was* Lilly staying around town this week, anyway? Had she broken up with the wealthy tennis pro? If Lilly moved back to town, I'd see her everywhere, because our town is too small to *not* see pretty much every resident about forty times a week.

I'd have to avoid the club, the Pub, the drugstore, and Gianni's restaurant (which I don't go to much anyway, but still). Forget that— I'd have to move. How dare Lilly drive me from my hometown!

Self-pity wasn't getting my paint job touched up, so I forced myself to toss aside my Lilly mini-obsession and deal with the can of pink paint before me. With renewed focus, I turned on the country music station and painted at marathon pace, ignoring my screaming shoulders and thinking ahead to possible store promotions. I could offer twenty percent off anything pink in the store for the rest of July, and serve up Bootsie's specialty cocktails every Friday afternoon.

"John knows ya usually go to bed real early!" Sophie said kindly. "Anyway, I'd help you finish that, but I can't get paint on these Stuart Weitzman slingbacks," Sophie told me, applying some lip gloss as she checked her phone.

"That's okay," I told her, "but thanks. I'm almost done. But Sophie, you know a lot about men and relationships . . . let me ask you something."

Sophie had put up with quite a bit of drama during her marriage to Barclay, and had accumulated some wisdom along the way.

"Do you think John would have a fling with Lilly? I mean, she had to have been at the club last night for that party?"

"Abso-freakin'-lutely he would!" Sophie said, staring at me. "I mean, John Hall's a nice guy, but that ex of his is stunning." Noticing my devastation, she tried to bolster me a bit.

"Listen, hon, I'm a realist. I don't think John had sex with Lilly last night, but ya might want to load on some makeup today and lose the Old Navy outfits now that he's back in town.

"Not that you don't look cute sometimes, too!" she added, which did little to improve my spirits. "Remember when you had those hair and eyelash extensions down in Florida? That looked good. And when Holly lends you her clothes, ya actually look stylish.

"One more piece of advice," she continued. "Ya need to get over to that country club. Your boyfriend just got back in town and he's probably checking out his gorgeous ex in a tight tennis dress as we speak."

Sophie has a way of bluntly but effectively laying out the core of an issue. I considered her words for about three seconds, then realized she was one hundred percent right. If paint touch-ups were needed, they could be done at 7 a.m. tomorrow before Bootsie arrived with the punch and the snacks for the reopening party.

Right now, it was time to get to the club.

"No offense," Sophie told me, whipping a dress, some sunglasses, and her makeup kit out of her purse, "but here's that caftan you had on the other day at Midnight Tony's. Put this on, add my Michael Kors shades, and let me swipe ya with my Benefit mascara and lip gloss. I'd take you to Ursula at Le Spa for the works, but we don't have time."

Chapter 19

JOE OUTLINED HIS plan while Bootsie and Gerda warmed up before heading out to the main court at the country club.

Gerda plus Bootsie made quite an intimidating doubles pair, I thought happily, as Gerda did hamstring stretches and Bootsie ran in place and did a ritual warm-up chant.

Holly sat next to me, sipping a Perrier. For her part, Sophie had decided to hit Le Spa and skip watching tennis.

I spied Lilly across the court, giving her an unnoticed evil glare from behind my borrowed fancy sunglasses. But I didn't see John anywhere at the club. A tiny ray of hope sparked within me—if John wasn't here to cheer on Lilly, that had to be a positive sign, didn't it?

"Here's the deal: I'm going to flatter Eula about her paintings, and then tell her I'm between jobs and want to do a two-hour makeover on her house," said Joe. "At no cost! Which, by the way, is my new concept for an HGTV show. With all the stuff my clients custom-order and then change their minds about, I've got three more storage units full of great furniture. I have, like thirty-five throw pillows, six lamps, and two Eames-style chairs in Holly's truck right now that are going to make Eula's place look fabulous!"

He did a *Godfather*-ish kiss of his hand to indicate the awesomeness of the storage locker contents. I gave Joe a closer look—how tipsy was he, exactly?

"One-day makeovers have been done to death," Bootsie observed, still jogging in place. "And what's the part of the plan that screws over Eula?"

"We search her house for that stupid *Heifer* painting while we do the makeover!" Joe screamed at her. "So shut up and get ready to ransack!"

"You and Eula don't like each other," I reminded him. "Why would she believe you want to redecorate her house? And maybe slow down on the medication. The tranquilizers seem to be making you *less* calm."

"I haven't started with the prescription meds yet," said Joe, a bit defensively. "This is vodka only. And trust me, Eula won't suspect anything. She's totally susceptible to flattery."

"That's true," Bootsie agreed. "I got Eula to help me plant Mummy's tulip beds last fall by telling her I've always admired her eye for spacing bulbs."

"Please," sniffed Joe. "Your mom's tulips were way too close together this spring. Bulbs need to breathe."

"I hate to say it," Bootsie said, "but I think Eula's going to take first prize next week with her SuperSauce Hybrids. She put some pics up on Instagram that were pretty impressive."

"There's another tomato contest in this town?" asked Joe in disbelief.

"All the late-ripening tomatoes will be judged next week,"

Holly explained. "And I can't believe I just said the words 'late-ripening tomatoes,'" she added.

"Some of the later categories are huge!" said Bootsie. "They don't call 'em Big Boys for nothing."

"You know what would be cool?" asked Joe. "If the world's largest tomato somehow smashed into Eula's face."

He did some quick searching on his phone and pushed his sunglasses up to read the screen. "The record is 8.41 pounds, grown by a guy in Minnesota. I mean, I'd settle for a three- or four-pounder to explode on Eula."

Holly's face brightened. "Can you send me that link?" she asked Joe.

"Anyway," I said, sensing that we were getting off topic, "don't forget that Bootsie needs to stop by the Binghams' house and find out more about Mega Wine Mart. And say you do get into Eula's house—maybe the painting's not even there! It could be at her office or something."

Where *was* John, anyway? Why hadn't he called me? I thought, watching Gerda bench-press a nearby Poland Spring dispenser.

"Eula doesn't have an office—we don't really have those at the *Gazette*," Bootsie said. "She shares a desk in the newsroom. Plus the painting is pretty big, and we only have seven hundred square feet of office space."

"If she has it, it's in her house," Joe said positively. "Eula's not good at things like stashing away stolen items. That's why she was a good class treasurer, and also, it's why she's no fun and needs to be sent on that two-year-long cruise."

As EXPECTED, BOOTSIE and Gerda emerged triumphant after seventy-five minutes of grueling tennis.

"You played great, Lilly," enthused Bootsie, which I found to be annoying. "Gerda and I had the height advantage, but you guys almost beat us."

"Your backhand is *so* Serena meets Venus mixed with vintage Navratilova," Lilly sang out to Bootsie and Gerda sweetly, appearing not to mind one bit that she and Eula had lost the championship.

Then again, why *would* Lilly care? She already had everything else going for her. Including, probably, an ex-husband who wanted her back.

Holly and I exchanged eye rolls as Bootsie, Gerda, Eula, and Lilly offered one another sporty compliments about how great they'd all played. Then again, since I don't play tennis and my main form of exercise is schlepping antiques and mowing my lawn, maybe this was standard procedure.

Finally, thankfully, there was a break in what was turning into an admiring verbal rehash of each point, and Joe leaped in.

"I never told you this, Eula, but I have an obsession with your house—I love it!" he said, with a slightly hysterical edge to his voice. "Those camellia bushes and the holly hedge and the French doors—the place screams English country village meets Umbrian farmhouse hideaway!"

"It does?" replied Eula, looking perplexed, flattered, and somewhat sweaty.

"You bet your sweet self it does," Joe told her. "It's close to perfect as it is, but I've got a really cool idea for an HGTV show where I do two-hour home makeovers that basically turn houses into the bricks-and-mortar equivalent of Jessica Alba blended with Cate Blanchett! I need pics of a couple of places this week for my pitch. I'm tentatively calling it *Extreme Makeover, Storage Locker Edition.*

"Let's go to your place right now! I've got rugs, pillows, and lamps in my truck right now, and this makeover can't wait an-other minute."

Eula hesitated for a minute, then finally agreed. "As long as you don't go upstairs," she said. "My attic's kind of a mess. I've been meaning to clean it out! Anyway, the door's locked."

"Of course, we won't go up there," said Bootsie. Her blue eyes were bulging happily. There's nothing Bootsie loves more than picking a lock, unless it's rooting through a medicine cabinet. I almost felt bad for Eula as I watched her depart, Joe and Bootsie on her heels.

"See you at my house at five-thirty to get ready for Gianni's super-secret event," said Holly, gathering up her bag and keys. Her toe was tapping and I noticed a large envelope of cash sticking out of her pristine beige Celine tote. "I might just go run a few er-rands. And do some organizing at home."

Errands? This could only mean one thing: shopping. Holly has Martha and Jared to do things like buy laundry detergent or pick up half-and-half. Shopping is a sign of distress with Holly. I mean, last summer she spent more than seven thousand dollars on bi-kinis that are still in the fancy Chanel bags they arrived in. That can't be healthy for anyone.

Also, when Holly starts "organizing," entire closets full of fan-tastic Theory outfits are sent to the Bryn Mawr Thrift Shop. This is great for the thrift shop, but seems a little impulsive. I should have known that Holly taking on three months of co-chairing with Eula meant she was in crisis.

"What with the Tomato Show, we haven't had a chance to catch up in a while," I told her. "And if you go to Saks—I mean, go run errands—you might run late, and miss Gianni's big announce-ment tonight." Honestly, if Holly went on a buying bender, she wouldn't be back till the luxury store closed at nine-thirty, or later, since they keep it open for her as long as she's still spending.

I noticed a slight eye twitch that for Holly indicated an emotional spiral.

"Howard's due back from Eugene soon, right?" I asked gently. "You must really miss him. But I hear Oregon is a beautiful place! Maybe you should fly out and spend a week!"

"I Googled Oregon," she told me, "and I don't think I get it."

"You don't get the whole state?"

"The only approved activities are fishing and hiking," she informed me. "Even Howard, who likes it there, said that's pretty much it."

I thought for a second, then remembered I'd had wine from Oregon once at the Pub.

"They have wineries!" I told her encouragingly. "That could be fun."

"I know of very strict spa out in Oregon," Gerda put in, as she zipped a tracksuit jacket on over her tennis outfit.

Holly perked up a little.

"This spa is run by Austrians," Gerda told her. "They give you, like, one kale smoothie a day and you get a handful of nuts at bedtime. The hikes are straight uphill for hours and they berate you till you cry if you don't keep up!

"You leave this place, your skin glowing and you weigh almost zero," Gerda added. "Maybe I go with you, Holly."

I could see Holly getting seriously interested. Despite her love of luxury, when Holly's depressed, she goes quickly from binge shopping to excessive working out and dining on a few sprigs of arugula. I sighed.

Who knows, maybe a week with Gerda would make Holly appreciate her cushy existence.

"What about phones and iPads?" Holly asked breathlessly. "I like the sound of the kale and the crying, but I might need access to technology."

"Austrians don't mind technology," Gerda told her. As if to prove this, her phone dinged, and she rooted through her tennis bag and eyed it.

"I had feeling Barclay was gonna be back today!" she barked. "Find My Friends alert me that he's heading back here on the A.C. Expressway. I gotta go. I gonna break my own rule and pick up a lot of booze and carbs for him so I can break the news that I'm opening new Pilates studio. I know Barclay—when I go out and get successful, he gonna be real mad."

BACK AT THE store, I hung up Sophie's caftan, put on my Bermuda shorts and Old Navy tank, and was about to head home with Waffles when Joe called.

"Nothing," said Joe when I answered. "Eula's got nothing incriminating in her house other than a bathrobe she stole from a W Hotel. Bootsie got into the attic, but it was just a bunch of musty old canvases. A few were painted over with Eula's version of, like, the *Mona Lisa*, but we didn't find Honey's painting."

"Could one of her *Mona Lisa*s have the real *Heifer* underneath Eula's paint job?" I asked.

"They were all much smaller, and none of the canvases we saw had a big gold frame like the one *Heifer* was in. Anyway, I've got to finish decorating Eula's living room in twelve minutes, so I gotta run," he said, and hung up.

I CHECKED MY phone for the millionth time that afternoon as I steered my rusty Subaru out of my driveway at five-thirty and turned toward Holly's place. I'd considered canceling on the Gianni event, but it sounded too depressing to stay home alone knowing my boyfriend was somewhere in town . . . and hadn't even bothered to pick up his dogs! All five mutts had eaten, run around the yard, and were back inside on the sofa, with the windows open to the summer breeze, but the gorgeous weather didn't do much for my mood.

Not even a text from John! He was probably clinking glasses right now with Lilly at her mom's fancy monogrammed house on Camellia Lane, caressing his ex's dewy, glowy cheekbones while they planned a tennis-themed wedding. Lilly would probably tell him he had too many dogs and they shed too much, and I'd end up having to adopt them all, spending the rest of my days alone but for a panting pack of beige fur.

And what about that drink Mike Woodford had mentioned? He could have called to make good on the offer he'd extended this morning, but so far my phone was completely silent.

My spirits lifted slightly when Holly's white Colonial house came into view after a lengthy meander down her driveway. Since she bought the place after old Mrs. Bingham died a couple of years back, she's had the Colketts installing roses, peonies, and hydrangeas in amazing profusion, and the result is spectacular.

Sure, I consoled myself as I pushed the gleaming doorbell, my boyfriend had been too busy playing tennis and hanging out with his ex-wife to call me, but at least I could be sure that Holly had a great outfit picked out for me to borrow while my heart crumbled into a million painful pieces.

"We're ready for ya!" sang Sophie as she opened Holly's door as soon as I rang. Behind her, Gerda nodded to me. "Just because you schlep antiques for a living doesn't mean you have to look like one!"

For her part, Sophie's tiny form was encased in a backless black silk frock that could only have been designed by Donatella Versace, her hair was swept up in the front in a poufy up-do, and she had on teetery six-inch gladiator heels.

For a girl who still hadn't wound up her divorce and might have broken up with her boyfriend, Sophie looked fabulous.

"How are you feeling?" I asked her. "Because you look great!"

"You know what, I'm doing awesome!" Sophie shrieked bravely. "Joe tried to stifle my mojo, and now I'm back and better than ever!"

I followed Sophie into Holly's minimalist foyer, which contains only a modern white light fixture, a low white marble table, and an expensive modern painting. The living room is similarly chic, which is why Howard has a clubby man cave in the basement where he can drink beer and eat nachos. Luckily for Howard, their housekeeper, Martha, cooks a lot of breakfasts and lunches when he's in town, since obviously Holly isn't going to make, say, pancakes. And fortunately for the rest of us, Martha loves to whip up magazine-worthy meals which Holly refuses to eat, so we get to enjoy amazing things like eggs Benedict on the patio all summer.

Actually it smelled like something fantastic was cooking in here right now . . . was there a *casserole* in the oven? I love casseroles! They're big around Bryn Mawr, and this one was emitting delicious aromas of chicken and cheese throughout Holly's art-gallery-looking house. Maybe Howard was coming home and Martha was baking said cheesy, carb-filled dish for him. This would be great news, since Holly's a lot calmer when Howard's around.

I quickly lost focus on the scent of baked goodness when I got upstairs to the guest room. There were three awesome dresses hanging on the closet door for me to choose between.

"I'd go with the slinkiest one," Sophie advised me. "'Cause I tried to tone down my outfits for Joe, and where did it get me? Exactly nowhere!"

With this, Sophie did a foot stamp and added a toss of her piled-up blond hair. "Plus all the Versace I had in my closet is back in business, starting tonight!"

TWENTY-FIVE MINUTES LATER, Sophie had aimed Holly's mega-watt blow-dryer at my hair with surprising skill, and was applying some kind of super-thick mascara that extended my eyelashes about two inches.

Holly, who had on an amazing white silk caftan, waved aside my protests about borrowing her clothes and told me that Gianni had insisted we get to his restaurant by six-thirty, and to hurry up and put on her pick for me, which was a Tibi yellow silk halter number.

"That dress is perfect for you," she told me. "On me, it looks like an omelette."

"It looks expensive—maybe you can return it!" I told her, feeling guilty about wearing her clothes for the millionth time. "I can take it to the Pack-N-Ship when I work next Sunday."

"Thanks, but I don't do returns," she told me airily. "Also, I've tried mailing things back at the Pack-N-Ship, and it never works. Last week, I ran into Leena at the Pub wearing a Phillip Lim cropped blouse I tried to send back weeks ago.

"She looked good in the shirt, though." Holly shrugged.

WE ARRIVED AT Gianni's restaurant to find two party buses idling outside and a crowd of well-dressed Gianni customers and investors climbing aboard.

No one was excited about the buses, especially since we didn't know where they were going. What if a two-hour schlep awaited us? I noticed that Gerda looked particularly leery as she tromped over in her BCBG jumpsuit and pair of Birkenstock sandals.

"I don't like buses," she announced.

"Come on, Gerda!" Sophie told her. "This is gonna be fun!"

"I don't like fun," Gerda said grimly.

"Sophie!" yelled Gianni, giving the Versace-clad girl a hug and managing to grab her tush in the process. "Holly! I got a fabulous night ahead for you girls. We going to special location for a fabulous dinner. Gianni has new business venture—out in the campagna!"

"Am I late?" said Bootsie, suddenly popping up at my elbow and scaring me.

"Don't sneak up like that!" I told her.

"I see trays of crab puffs being carried onto those party buses," Bootsie told us.

Just then, I noticed waiters carrying big silver buckets of iced champagne onto the idling vehicles.

"Let's go!" yelled Bootsie.

Chapter 20

FORTY MINUTES LATER, the tipsy crowd piled out of the two buses and onto the stone walkway of a beautiful, tiny stone farmhouse.

We'd headed west for two exits on the Turnpike, then due north on a winding country road that also headed to my fave Chester County flea market, Stoltzfus's.

Luckily, Gianni himself had jumped onto the first bus, while Bootsie, Sophie, and I rode in the second vehicle. Luckily, just a few miles off the Turnpike, the buses turned right and braked to a halt on the long, oak-lined driveway of a pretty stone farmhouse. The sun was setting, but a few artfully placed spotlights illuminated the tall trees around us, and dozens of strings of white party lights hung from branches above two long white-clothed tables set with Mason jars filled with white roses and peonies, and about seven hundred white votive candles.

"Hey everybody, I going to make a speech now!" said the chef, who was waiting at the head of the driveway, the waiters and party staff assembled in black and white outfits behind him.

All the guests looked askance at the prospect of a monologue by Gianni, who isn't known for brevity. However, things looked up when four waiters started quickly handing everyone glasses of tasty-looking red wine. Thankfully, the speech itself was on the short side.

"*Benvenuti* to Gianni's new business venture!" said the chef, his bald dome glinting in the glow of the candles. "And hey, look back there, past that rose garden behind me." He indicated some buoyant bushes in full pink and red bloom about twenty feet in the direction of the little stone house and a barn. "The Colketts put those roses in today, and by the way, Colketts, you mess up! That's not enough bushes, I told you to do like four hundred roses, you guys fucked up again! Anyway," he continued, while the Colketts' faces turned from proud to crestfallen, "Gianni got big announcement. Already I having a great year with new restaurant and hit show on Food Network, and I meet a lot of celebrities and probably gonna join Leonardo DiCaprio's posse on his yacht next summer! But tonight, I got different news.

"Behind the rose garden is pasture, and you see animals in it?"

We all peered through the dusk, and small faces with wide-set eyes, huge ears, long noses, and a sweet and slightly sleepy expression were visible, lined up along a wood fence. They resembled in stature a good-size dog, but appeared to be . . . Wait, were those . . . They kept nibbling the grass, munching the wood of the fence, and were sticking their heads through to try to eat the roses . . .

"Gianni is starting an artisanal goat cheese farm," shouted the chef. "These little suckers gonna make thirty-eight-dollar-a-pound goat cheese for Gianni. Gonna be my greatest moneymaker yet!"

"SOPHIE! KRISTIN! OVER here," sang out Tim Colkett, who was adjusting some huge orange trees in terracotta pots over by an outdoor bar. The fresh cocktail in his hand had apparently numbed the sting of the chef's diss about his rose garden, and the Colketts looked back to their usual upbeat selves.

And honestly, the setting was so delightful that it immediately lifted the mood. A jazz trio was playing under a grove of birch trees, sous-chefs were hovering over a grill that was currently occupied by huge hunks of fragrant meats, and waiters were passing tiny crab-and-chevre puffs.

The scene was honestly pretty spectacular. I had to hand it to Gianni—the man knew how to throw a party.

"Did we do an amazing job with this place or what?" said Tom Colkett, giving us all hugs. "There was nothing here this morning but grass and goats. Seriously, we've outdone ourselves—again!"

"Did you notice the orchids and lanterns suspended from the sycamores in the manner of a free-form sculpture?" added Tim. "It's the newest thing in flower design. Fruits, vegetables, candles, you name it—if you can wrap it in twine and dangle it from a branch, or a fence, you've basically nailed that whole *InStyle* back of the magazine, celebrity party thing. I mean, would Sofia Vergara have a party without orchids *à la branche*? I don't think so."

"The other genius trend we've basically invented—well, maybe we weren't the absolute first to do this, but we were early adopters—is the party shed," Tom informed us.

"Voilà!" He pointed to what seemed like a place to store rakes—a cute wood and stone structure that might have been a spring house in an earlier incarnation—and flung open the door. "You're welcome!"

The shed was also lit entirely by candles and lanterns, and was totally adorable, if something of a fire hazard. A long barn table had been turned into a bar with charming antique glassware and pots of herbs lining shelves behind it, where a hot bartender flashed a handsome grin as he muddled mint in a glass pitcher. The party shed had its own Latin soundtrack, and a sexy, stylish vibe, as if Martha Stewart, J. Lo, and one of the Iglesias family of singers were cohosting a barbecue.

"The only problem is the actual goats," said Tim, turning more serious. "My aunt in Vermont kept goats, so I know a lot about ruminant animals. I tried to explain to Gianni that goats eat *everything*. Roses, fences, hydrangeas, tires, furniture—they'll mow it right down."

"We discouraged him from investing a lot in flowering plants, which are pricey," Tom agreed. "But he didn't listen, and he insisted on a twenty-eight-hundred-dollar outdoor sofa from Restoration Hardware." He shrugged nervously. "We put an eight-foot deer fence up between the pasture and the house, but I already saw a few goats starting to chew it."

"Hi there," said a familiar voice. We all turned to see a girl wearing beige and a smug expression, with a notepad and pencil in hand.

"We just did a forty-five-minute interview with her," whispered Tom, grabbing Tim and taking a left turn toward the bar. "See ya!"

"Hey, Eula," said Bootsie. "I didn't see you on the party bus."

"That's because I'm here working," Eula informed her. "On a *Gazette* story about Gianni's chevre business! When you guys were redoing my living room today, I stopped by the newspaper office and the press release had just come in about this place. So here I am! Look for my byline tomorrow," she added breezily, turning on her heel to go interview the Binghams.

"When is that Powerball drawing?" asked Bootsie, grabbing another drink from a passing waiter. "Because I'm starting to think if Eula doesn't win and leave town, I might need to do something that will land me in prison."

"Hey, there's Abby from the club," Sophie said, pointing out the long blond curls of the cute waitress, who was out of country-club uniform tonight and into a sexy black knit dress topped with a tiny white apron. She was passing a tray of crab salad on a grilled polenta round topped with—what else?—goat cheese.

"Abby!" Bootsie called out, beckoning the girl over. "You're working for Gianni now?"

Abby looked distinctly uncomfortable, and a guilty expression appeared on her pretty face.

"Um, just for tonight!" she said, handing Bootsie a cocktail napkin along with the polenta. "And I might do some part-time waitressing for him, if I can make it work with my club schedule." She looked poised to take off, but she was too late, because Bootsie was aiming a laserlike stare at her that I was all too familiar with.

"You're not, you know, getting horizontal with Chef Gianni, are you?" Bootsie asked Abby.

Bootsie's got a weirdly accurate radar for even the most unlikely romantic entanglements, but in this case, I was worried about the same thing. Abby was far too cute for Gianni to have hired for her food service skills.

"No!" said Abby, looking embarrassed. "We just, you know, had some wine the other night, and he, um, asked me out to dinner. And to work at this party!"

"How old are ya?" asked Sophie. "Is it legal for him to date you, because that's super creepy if you're a teenager, and your parents would be real upset."

"I'm twenty-one," said Abby proudly. "But we haven't . . . you know."

Bootsie raised a skeptical eyebrow.

"Okay, I kissed Gianni the other night, but that's all we did, and then he told me he could get me on his TV show!"

She paused for a second, looking nervous. "You won't tell my parents, will you?" she said to Bootsie. "Plus I have a boyfriend at school!"

"We won't say anything," Holly told her. "But let me save you some trouble. Within three weeks, Gianni will be dating at least two other girls who work at his Beverly Hills restaurant, and he'll have you down at the airport bribing customs officials to bring in illegal salami. You need to go back to school and forget the TV show."

"Okay," said Abby, looking relieved. "I was getting stressed out about moving to L.A., anyway. It's really expensive there!" She paused nervously. "I guess I'll tell Gianni tomorrow night that I can't see him anymore. We're supposed to have dinner at his restaurant."

"You might want to cancel that," Sophie advised. "Take it from me, and I had to pay a life coach ten grand to figure this out, once you realize you're in a toxic relationship, you need to take the nearest exit ramp. I mean, I'm friends with Gianni and everything, but he's too old for a nice girl like you."

"I hear what you're saying." Abby nodded earnestly. "But it's just one meal, and to be honest, I've never been to Ristorante Gianni, and I'm dying to go! Gianni wants me to try some new spicy lobster pasta and some fancy one-hundred-fifty-dollar bottle of wine. I mean, I'm in college. When am I ever going to get to try something like that? I'll dump him right after dinner!"

"*SOPHIEEE!*" SANG OUT Lobster Phil.

"Phil!" Sophie greeted her old friend, "What are you doing in Amish country?"

"I'm here as both guest and business partner," he told us, munching a cucumber-radish-goat cheese hors d'oeuvre. "My associate Sweet Freddie McDonald and I are minor investors in Gianni's business empire.

"You're all looking beautiful tonight," he added. Phil did have excellent manners, and a certain gallant style that was very endearing.

"Thanks!" Sophie told him. "I wouldn't have pictured you putting your money into goats."

"This is just between us, but Sweet Freddie wants to take the Vegas hotel and restaurants in a new direction," Phil said. "We're going less Jersey, and more upscale foodie. In fact, we're sponsoring the Fall Food Classic in Vegas, which gets all the celebrity chefs and is huge for prestige! Freddie says he wants the place to be more than just a drinks-and-slots kind of place. I mean, obviously we'll still be both of those, but we're determined to take our place to the next level.

"We're going to launch our new restaurant in September during the Fall Food Classic, and wait till ya hear the concept."

We all fell silent, thinking. Holly and Sophie have invested in restaurants before, but honestly, none of us knows much about culinary trends, and as a group, we can't cook.

"Is it some kind of fusion food, like Southern cuisine meets South of France?" guessed Sophie. "Like, grits and cheddar biscuits combined with, like, steak frites?"

"Fusion would be fun," offered Holly. "There's that one place in Vegas that combines Asian and Spanish cuisines, and it's got really cute lacquered red walls and delicious tequila drinks. Is your new restaurant, um, Moroccan meets Mexican?"

"I'm guessing all smoothies," said Gerda. "Everything is vegetable or fruit in a blender. That would be new in Las Vegas."

"Maybe the food gets delivered by Magic Mike guys," said Bootsie. "That's what I would do if I were you, Phil. Or how about this: Strip on the Strip. And you get girls in bikinis to serve strip steaks!"

"I like where you're going with that," Phil told Bootsie, "but what Freddie wants to do is way more upscale." He paused for effect.

"It's gonna be organic! And Gianni's goat cheese is going to be the theme of the Food Classic's opening night! That's a three-day event kicked off with a party for twenty thousand people at the Vegas Convention Center!"

He beamed at us proudly as we all pondered this silently. The Food Classic did sound like a really big deal. I mean, I had heard of it only because Sophie had pointed it out in the magazine at Le Spa, but still, they had promoted the weekend in a prominent spread, and any event that attracts that many people is obviously popular. Still though—organic? Given my minestrone-from-a-can level of kitchen prowess, I'm not one to judge current food trends. It seemed, even to me, that organic fare wasn't the newest culinary trend around.

"Organic food is gonna be everywhere at the Classic," Phil added helpfully. "You know, organic chickens, organic meats, arugula and shit like that grown without chemicals."

"Organic's been done to death," Bootsie told him, chugging her drink. I gazed at her with some alarm. Probably dissing a possible Vegas mafia casino owner's big idea wasn't a great idea, especially out in Amish country, where there are thousands of acres under which a six-foot-tall blond tennis player's body could disappear forever, sowed into a field of pumpkins.

"Not in Vegas!" Phil told her, seemingly unoffended. "And not in my and Freddie's place."

"It sounds real awesome!" said Sophie kindly. "And a real crowd-pleaser. I mean, even in Vegas, people like to think they're doing something healthy."

"I approve," seconded Gerda.

"How about I meet you after the party tonight, and you show me where the Wine Mart is gonna go?" Phil suggested. "Nine p.m. back at the restaurant?" Sophie agreed, and Phil excused himself and headed to the bar.

"I couldn't help overhearing what that guy was telling you," whispered Abby a few minutes later. "And you didn't hear this from me, but the goat cheese in these pastry puffs isn't organic, even though Gianni's claiming the cheese from this farm is all-natural. We got it from, like, five different supermarkets today! Half the staff had to go buy up every package of chevre in a three county radius!"

"What, Gianni didn't have enough cheese?" asked Bootsie.

"He had nothing! The goats aren't producing milk," said Abby. "They've been here a week and from one hundred and fifty goats, he hasn't produced an ounce of cheese. The goats are on strike or something! Oh, hi, Mr. Woodford," she added to another guest as she headed back to pick up more hors d'oeuvres.

"Hey there," said Mike to me. "I wanted to tell you what Eula was doing with that wheelbarrow this morning. She uses compost from Sanderson cows on her rose hedges I see her hit the barn and wheel it out once a week, minimum."

"What!" said Bootsie. "She steals your cow manure?"

"It's an unspoken agreement," Mike told her. "We have a lot of it."

"That burns my ass," fumed Bootsie. "First she grows tomatoes in Jersey, then she's got cow product from the fanciest estate in town. No wonder her roses look so good."

"I didn't know ya were a fan of Gianni's," Sophie piped up, giving Mike the once-over. "Ya look good in that navy blazer," she told him. "If I wasn't so in love with my decorator boyfriend, I'd have a crush on you. But I know you used to fool around with Kristin here, so I could never have a fling with you."

"When I heard Gianni was opening a cheese business, I had to see for myself." Mike grinned down at Sophie. "I think he might find farming to be a real challenge."

I was distracted by his tan. And the beard stubble. Did he grow it on purpose?

I moved a little closer to inhale a whiff of Irish Spring . . . Mike didn't have any gorgeous ex-wives, unlike my boyfriend, or maybe former boyfriend . . . maybe I should just give up on John!

Then again, I had all those dogs at my house right now, and it probably wouldn't be possible to make out with Mike with Waffles plus four wagging, slobbering mutts in residence.

At that moment, I noticed a tall, lean form over by the goat herd in jeans and a polo shirt. He bent over to scratch a nanny goat behind her ears, and my jaw dropped.

Our eyes met and he broke into a smile as he opened the wooden gate and wrapped me in a huge hug.

I hugged him back, then stepped back and looked at him. Before I could think it through, I opened my mouth and uttered the whiny words no girl should ever say: "Why haven't you called me?"

JOHN EXPLAINED THAT he'd been almost back to Bryn Mawr yesterday afternoon when he got a last-minute call from his chiropractor to play in the doubles tournament after the guy's original partner had dropped out, and with the match starting at 7 p.m. and then everyone staying afterward at the club to eat, it had been after ten. "I was about to text you last night and come over when Gianni called and said he had an emergency situation, and begged me to come out here to check on his goats," he explained.

He'd followed Gianni to this patch of Amish farmland and examined the sleepy animals, while Gianni cursed everything on a cloven hoof and bemoaned his herd's lack of productivity. "It was close to 1 a.m. when I got back to Bryn Mawr, and I know you're never up that late," he finished. "Gianni had me here most of the day today, too, and when he told me about the party tonight, I knew you'd be here. I thought I'd surprise you."

I digested all this for a minute.

"Are you ready to go?" said John, putting his arm around me. "We can go pick up the dogs and go to my place."

Miserably, I looked at him, trying to sift through my trust issues and Lilly Merriwether worries. Could anyone be this caught up in veterinary medicine . . . and think it was a good idea to be back in town for more than twenty-four hours and not call your girlfriend?

"Thanks for letting the dogs stay with you!" he said. "You're the best to take care of them."

That did it. I did love John's dogs, but I was tired of being covered in dog hair, and sick of fretting about him and Lilly. I needed a night to think things over. Maybe I *couldn't* handle dating a guy who was this devoted to his work and had a perfect ex-wife. Also, dogs are the best, but does anyone really need four?

A small voice of reason deep within me pointed out that I spent most of my time at work, too, and the majority of my spare time with Bootsie, Holly, and Sophie. I probably needed to focus more energy on John.

I was irrationally upset and didn't have the energy to sort

through the millions of emotions rocketing around inside my borrowed Tibi dress, so I informed John with a chilly hauteur that I'd promised Bootsie and Sophie to go look at old Mrs. Bingham's garden shack with a guy named Lobster Phil LaMonte tonight. He could pick up his pack of dogs in the morning.

As we all got back on the party buses, a whiff of something that wasn't quite as pleasantly scented as the espresso and biscotti that Gianni's staff had just passed around floated our way. Holly wrinkled her perfect nose, while Sophie gave a loud sniff. I actually found the smell somewhat pleasant, but I like a nice earthy scent, and I live across from Sanderson, so farm odors are pretty familiar. At least the new rose garden was also wafting out its own heavenly scent.

"Smells like goat," pronounced Bootsie. As if to confirm this, the herd started bleating loudly. They seemed scared by the loud bus motors and the tipsy guests scrambling on board.

"Shut up, you *putana* goats!" Gianni yelled as the bus doors slammed shut.

Chapter 21

PHIL TOLD US he'd meet us back at Ristorante Gianni, since he was a town car guy and didn't do buses. We all climbed into his huge black sedan forty-five minutes later for a quick tour de Bryn Mawr.

"So where's the Mega Wine Mart gonna be?" Phil asked.

"We're heading there now!" said Sophie. "Sorry it's so dark out, but if you look past those pastures, you can see we're passing a real fancy estate called Sanderson, which is where that lady who got her painting stolen lives." Phil look duly impressed at the size and scope of Mrs. Potts's estate, and kept driving.

"Did we tell ya we got a name on the developer of the Wine Mart?" she added. "Some guy named Barry Tutto. We can't get a phone number for him, though! It's like he doesn't exist in real life."

"Barry Tutto," repeated Phil. "That has a familiar ring to it. I'll look into it for you."

"Here's where the Mega Wine Mart is gonna be!" said Sophie, indicating the driveway that led through the woods toward old

Mrs. Bingham's former garden store. A summer moon illuminated the lofty trees.

"These woods are fabulous," said Phil, rolling down his window and sniffing the breeze. "Just smell that fresh night air. This is freakin' beautiful."

"It won't be for long," Bootsie told him. "See that old building? That's going to be a boutique wine store, but that's just for like a month, and then it's big box all the way."

BACK AT GIANNI's restaurant, Phil insisted on going in and buying us yet one more drink. To my relief, the chef himself was nowhere to be found.

"You were just at his party, right?" asked the hostess. "Is it true that the place smelled like goat?"

"Just for the last five minutes," Bootsie told her.

"Better than nothing," said the girl, who added that she was clocking out and took off. Ristorante Gianni was winding down for the night, with diners paying their bills and heading out. I was already wishing I was in bed. It seemed, though, that Lobster Phil wasn't someone you disappeared on—unless he wanted you to.

"That Sanderson is something special," Phil mused now, after throwing a stack of twenties onto the bar. "Mrs. Potts's house is sparking all kinds of ideas in me."

"Like what?" said Bootsie. "Are you a fan of cows? Because that's her main interest."

"I'm thinking old England," he said, swirling his drink. "It's a totally new concept for a Vegas restaurant and lounge. Imagine this: paneling, old paintings, old rugs, huge sofas, all that. And, like, roast beef and peas for the food, and waiters in '60s Rat Pack–style suits. *Downton Abbey* meets *Ocean's 11*."

"I thought ya loved the Vegas vibe," Sophie said to Phil. "You got all those great places to eat and shop, and look at your tan—it's awesome."

"True," allowed Phil. "But I grew up in Jersey. Sometimes I miss the trees and the forest. There's not a single tree in Vegas unless you count some palm trees they plunked down around the pools at the casinos. I mean, I was never a tree-hugger back when I lived in Atlantic City, but you knew they were just a couple exits up the Garden State Parkway if you wanted them."

"Maybe ya should move back!" encouraged Sophie. "At least spend the summers here at the shore?"

"No way," said Phil. "Not with Diana-Maria still living there. Plus I'm Sweet Freddie's main guy in Vegas now."

"Who's Sweet Freddie?" asked Bootsie.

"Sweet Fred McDonald is an associate of Gianni and Barclay from when they worked in Jersey," Sophie told us. "He's from the non-Italian part of their, you know, business consortium." She paused for a moment, seemingly lost in thought.

"Didn't you guys do some art sales, too, back in the day, Phil?" she asked her old friend. "I mean, I know Barclay and you did construction and trucking, and a buncha other businesses, but I think I remember my ex telling me that you're a real art lover! You and Sweet Freddie had, like, a gallery out in Vegas a few years back, didn't ya?"

"Just for a few months," Phil told her smoothly.

"Why'd ya close it?" persisted Sophie.

"We had a few visits from Customs and Border Protection," Phil said, not warming to the subject. "Those guys are real picky about where a painting comes from. I didn't have time to spend months researching, like, the last twelve owners of every picture we sold, so we closed up shop."

"I remember ya had a lot of antique pictures at your place in Jersey!" Sophie said. "Real nice ones, too. Lot of outdoor scenes."

Bootsie seemed to be missing the fact that Phil was a fan of the exact kind of painting stolen from Mrs. Potts, and the fact that he'd actually been in the art business until he'd been shut down for not authenticating the provenance of the paintings he sold. She was still stuck on a possible family connection to the aforementioned Sweet Freddie.

"We have some cousins named McDonald on Mummy's side. Maybe I'm related to Sweet Freddie," said Bootsie.

"I doubt it," said Sophie, shaking her head. "You don't resemble Sweet Freddie even a little bit. He's real short, and real mean. All of the other guys were always gentlemen, except of course my dumb ex Barclay and Sweet Freddie. One time Freddie ripped off a guy's fingernails and Krazy Glued them to his front door."

"I don't think he's one of Mummy's cousins," agreed Bootsie.

Just then, Joe walked in, wearing his typical Bryn Mawr–in–July outfit of crisp striped shirt, a preppy green belt, and khaki shorts.

"Honey Bunny, this is Phil LaMonte from Vegas!" shrieked Sophie. "Phil, this is my almost-fiancé Joe Delafield, who's a decorator and is *mega*-talented. He even designed a dining room down in Magnolia Beach, Florida, that was featured in *Elle Decor!*" I couldn't help noticing that Phil was roughly three times the size of Joe. His hand resembled a baseball mitt when he shook Joe's much smaller paw.

"I also do renovations," said Joe, who stood up straight to his full height, which put him at chest level with Phil.

Thankfully, since it was nighttime, he wasn't carrying his usual tote bag of fabric samples and paint chips. I wasn't sure Phil would be able to understand Joe's passion for perfectly decorated rooms—though, who knows, maybe he could? You don't make it as far as Phil had in the restaurant business without an eye for good design.

"Joe just ripped out a kitchen in Florida and totally rebuilt it," I explained to Phil, since I wasn't sure Sophie had presented her boyfriend in the best possible light. Probably referencing construction rather than *Elle Decor* was the way to go.

"It was a complete gut job. Joe's great on a job site!" I added.

"That's real interesting," Phil said politely. "Well, you're a lucky guy, Joe. Sophie's a sweetheart. Nice to meet you."

With that, Phil took off for his hotel in A.C., while Joe gingerly seated himself on the bar stool Phil had just vacated. I could see him barely restraining himself from dusting it off with a cocktail napkin.

"So that guy was one of Barclay's good friends?" he asked Sophie, striving for a neutral tone as he waved down the bartender for a Stoli. I felt a bit badly for Joe. Between Gerda's return from Florida and spending weeks on end arguing about potholders with Mrs. Earle, he wasn't exactly having a fantastic summer. Plus Joe's secure in who he is, but any one of Sophie's former Jersey friends could squash him like a bug, which has to be unsettling

"Lobster Phil's basically the king of Vegas these days," Bootsie informed him. "I did a little Googling earlier, and the guy has, like, not only his restaurant, but owns most of the casino it's in, plus does retail and liquor on the side. I think he's got a little crush on Sophie, too!"

"Ya think?" said Sophie, looking excited. "He always did like me! It used to really annoy his girlfriend Diana-Maria. He once gave me a Gucci suitcase for my birthday. It was real sweet of him.

Which, by the way, is coming up in three weeks. My birthday, that is." Here, she gave Joe a little hug and squeeze, and dangled her ring-free left hand in front of his tumbler of vodka.

"We could get Phil to take us up to Trenton to see some of his jeweler buddies," she told Joe. "Or go to Vegas! He probably knows all the best diamond guys in Vegas, and you know they have huge rocks there! People probably have to pawn their wives' good stuff all the time out there."

Joe, who rarely breaks a sweat, stood up, a sheen of perspiration on his tastefully tanned forehead, and Bootsie and I exchanged "uh-oh" glances. I noticed his hands were trembling and an eyelid was twitching.

"Sophie, I've given in on Versace plates and painting your shoe closet gold," he said through clenched teeth. "I don't even care anymore that you force me to watch *American Horror Story: Hotel* with Lady Gaga even though you know that show terrifies me.

"But I'm not going to live in the same house as Gerda, and I'm definitely not going to buy a ring from a pawnbroker in a strip mall in Vegas!"

"Ya don't have to be so snooty about a preowned rock!" shrieked Sophie. "You're always blabbing about how great antiques are. What are antiques except a fancier way of saying 'used,' anyway? If desks and chandeliers can be used by some old folks in the 1800s, how come a ring from those guys on *Pawn Stars* isn't an antique, too?"

I thought she had a point, but didn't think it would be wise to voice an opinion. Plus a lot of what I sell at The Striped Awning doesn't meet Joe's standards for antiques, either, so it's a bit of a touchy subject with me.

"Because it isn't! A ring once worn by a Real Housewife probably isn't all that old!" Joe screamed back.

Clearly, he'd gone too far, because the normally sweet-tempered Sophie turned pink with rage, grabbed her gold Versace clutch bag, and made for the door. Her exit was quite effective, I thought admiringly.

Unfortunately, she hadn't driven to Gianni's, so she was forced to turn around and come back to the bar, where Joe was gathering up his phone and making for the door, too. "I need a ride home," she told Bootsie, a huge tear dropping down on her tiny face.

"Don't worry, *I'm* leaving," said Joe. "And I'm going to stay in Holly's guest room tonight."

"Good!" Sophie told him, looking sadder than I'd ever seen her. I gulped sadly, and followed a tearful Sophie and an uncomfortable Bootsie out to the parking lot.

Maybe this really was the end of the unlikely Joe-and-Sophie pairing. Opposites attract, clearly, but were there differences finally pushing them too far apart?

Chapter 22

A GENTLE KNOCK on my back door woke me up at seven-thirty the next morning. I peeked from my window, and saw John Dogs exploded out of my bedroom, hurtling down the stairs, barking and wagging in a frenzy of joy at reuniting with their owner, and after I showered and got dressed, we all piled into his huge SUV.

"We'll ride out to Gianni's farm, get breakfast, and I'll drop you back at The Striped Awning before lunch," John told me. "And even though you haven't invited me, I'm coming to your reopening party this afternoon. I'll bartend!"

"Great!" I said, instantly forgiving him.

I mean, how many guys will adopt every stray mutt in town and serve drinks at your antiques store party? He'd picked up Starbucks, too. I needed to forget about Lilly Merriwether. This guy was a keeper.

AS WE PULLED up to Gianni's farm, two Amish men in hats and simple clothing were waiting in the driveway, and greeted John with handshakes. Gianni, for his part, emerged from his farmhouse shaking his fist at the pasture.

"These *putana* goats still doing nothing for me!" he told John. "We got, like, two drops of milk today. Plus they eating everything!"

As predicted by the Colketts, overnight the goats had chewed through the fencing, mowed down the hydrangeas to stubs, and started in on the cushions for the outdoor sofas on Gianni's patio.

"These *caprino* a real pain in the ass!" Gianni raged. "They defective!"

"Goats don't respond well to yelling and stress," John told the chef. "Which is why I asked the Stoltzfuses here to help you out, Chef."

"You guys from that flea market?" Gianni asked the two men suspiciously.

"We're cousins of the owners," one answered.

"Trust me, Chef, this will work out better for everyone," John said reassuringly. "You can go back to what you do best—restaurants—and your goats will start producing a ton of great cheese."

"Okay," agreed Gianni. "Maybe that work better for Gianni. You're hired," he told the two men, who nodded and headed toward the goat pasture, making a gentle clucking noise as they opened the gate.

The herd ran joyfully toward the farmers, and we were about to leave when a black town car pulled up and a man in a sport coat emerged from the backseat.

"Lobster Phil!" I said, waving. I paused when I saw the expression on Phil's face as he walked toward Gianni. He didn't look like usual charming self.

"We need to talk," he told the chef. "I've come across some information that gives me a lot of concerns about this goat place, and also another business I think you're trying to sneak past me and Sweet Freddie."

"Uh, now not a good time," said Gianni nervously, indicating the Stoltzfuses. "These guys my new employees, and I got to meet with them."

Phil paused, shading his eyes to observe the gamboling goats and their new management.

"I see you're lucky again," he told Gianni. "I got respect for Amish people, so I'm leaving. We'll talk later," he added grimly.

BOOTSIE WAS GLUGGING Paul Masson brandy into her mom's punch bowl while John added ginger ale, seltzer, and fresh peach slices when Leena arrived at The Striped Awning that afternoon.

"Hey, there," Leena said. "Looks like this reopening's going to be a real blowout!"

"Any news about that missing package?" asked Bootsie, making a neat free throw with the empties into my recycling bin.

"Nothing yet," said Leena, unconcerned. "That's working in the mail business for you, though! If I lost sleep over every package that got sidetracked, I'd be in the wrong line of work."

"Uh-huh," I said, thinking that this explained a lot. "Have some peach punch, Leena," I added. "Thanks for coming."

"Sure," said Leena. "By the way, Kristin, I brought you something." She whipped a bright red shirt out of her handbag. "It's a Pack-N-Ship polo in your size! I noticed that you took one of my uniforms the other day, and I wanted to tell you it's okay!" She added an understanding wink. "The shirt you took is probably too big for you. You can bring it back anytime."

"Um—thanks," I said, glaring at Bootsie. "That's really nice of you."

"I'm out of here," said Joe, seeing Eula park her Miata across the street, and Honey Potts steering an old station wagon into the no-parking zone in front of my shop.

"Don't leave," I implored as a group including Skipper, Holly, George Fogle, Officer Walt, and the Colketts arrived, and Eula swung through the front door behind them. "Please help me with Eula and Mrs. Potts. And at least stay long enough to brag to the Colketts that you gave this place its makeover!"

"Five minutes," Joe agreed, gulping down some peach punch. He straightened his shoulders and plastered on a charming smile, while I sent thankful glances his way.

"Mrs. Potts!" he said. "And Eula. Don't you both look absolutely *gorgeous* today!"

"So PEOPLE BUY this kind of old stuff?" asked Mrs. Potts, apparently stymied as she eyed old crystal decanters on trays and embroidered footrests, looking her usual tanned, outdoorsy self in knee-length green shorts and a crisp shirt. "'Cause these are the sort of knickknacks I'm always giving away to the town rummage sale."

"Half the store's probably from your attic!" Joe agreed. "This one"—here, he indicated me—"gets all the stuff for this antiques store at flea markets, and out of the back of a van from some hippies out in Lancaster County."

"And you can make a living that way?" Honey asked with evident surprise, taking a suspicious sip of punch. She plunked it down on a silver tray and asked for a vodka, which Joe gallantly supplied.

"Not really," Joe told her. "I mean, Kristin's working part-time at the Pack-N-Ship, too, so that pretty much says it all."

"I give ya credit for trying." Mrs. P. shrugged. "I'll call Holly next time I'm doing a clean-out, and you can have first pick."

"Thank you!" I told her gratefully as the Honey picked up a monogrammed serving spoon, inspected it, shook her head doubtfully, and made for the door—but not before Bootsie aimed a question at her.

"Any word on your painting?" Bootsie asked. "*Heifer*'s still missing, right, Mrs. P.?"

Bootsie must have had a few servings of peach punch already, I realized, since this wasn't a question most people would lob at the town's preeminent doyenne. Honey's expression turned more sour than usual, and she shook her head as she exchanged good-byes with George and Holly.

"Walt's been doing his best, and George here has called everyone and their uncle in art circles from New York to Paris, so I still believe *Heifer* will be back," she said, making a dignified exit.

"That makes one of us," said Joe. "Hey, guys," he added to Tim and Tom, who were eyeing the pink, brown, and modern-meets-antique decor of my store. "Just to give you some background, I took a store full of crapola antiques and a single can of paint and gave this place its Palm Springs–meets–Provence cool factor. In *one* day," he added smugly.

"Cute," said Tim dismissively. "It's really got that roadside-shack-turned-convenience-store vibe."

"Remember that time we were coming back from an antiques show in Massachusetts and our car broke down, and the guy who towed us out of the ditch sold both antiques and homemade beef jerky out of his garage?" Tom asked him. "This kind of reminds me of that place."

Joe's eyes bulged angrily, but before he had a chance to formulate a Colkett-aimed insult, Holly gently steered him to the back seating area, grabbing George and me on the way.

"I have a plan that will keep Sophie happy and buy you some time while you work on your commitment issues," Holly informed Joe. "George has a connection for a ring that would be perfect for Sophie as preengagement bling. Something that's flashy enough for Sophie, but doesn't weigh more than she does."

"I'm nodding." Joe nodded.

"I got a call from some guy who says he was a driver on the Lady Gaga–Tony Bennett Cheek to Cheek Tour," George told us. "He has an amethyst ring that Lady Gaga wore one night onstage, and he sent me a picture. Let me find it in my phone," he added, scrolling through e-mails.

"Is it stolen?" asked Joe, alarmed.

"No, it's not *stolen*," George informed him. "Well, it probably isn't. This driver guy claims a lot of items from the tour were sold to benefit charity, and he got a good deal on it."

"Anyway, the guy's girlfriend broke up with him, so he's selling it for five hundred dollars, since it's impossible to prove that Lady Gaga actually ever wore it," Holly told Joe. "But if you mention the Gaga connection to Sophie, she'll stop bothering you about those rings she saw in *Town & Country*."

Joe eyed George's phone skeptically, and I took a look over his shoulder. The ring featured an oval-shaped lavender stone framed by tiny diamonds in a simple, elegant setting.

"It's nice," said Joe grudgingly.

"It comes with a signed Lady Gaga photo," Holly told him. "This is your best shot at getting Sophie to be almost-engaged."

I knew Holly was right. When it comes to celebrities, the ring's possible previous owner is Sophie's hands-down favorite, especially since the glamorous singer posed for Versace ads.

This plan was a guaranteed win—if Joe was willing to almost-commit to Sophie.

"I'm thinking," said Joe.

"While you think, you might want to head out the back if you want to avoid your possible fiancée right now," Holly told him. "She and Gerda just parked in the loading zone in front."

"So, EULA, I hear you're doing some painting these days," said George forty-five minutes and two peach punches later. George isn't much of a drinker, and he seemed a little sauced.

"Eula did some nice still-life paintings for the Tomato Show," I told George. "I have a few of them here to sell," I added, then wished I hadn't as I remembered Joe telling me he'd shoved them in my storage room. It's rare that I feel badly for Eula, but there was so much hate in the room for her that I had to say something positive.

"Where *are* my paintings?" asked Eula. "'Cause I don't see them hanging anywhere in the shop."

"Um—I'm saving them for when I officially reopen tomorrow!" I improvised. "I know they're going to sell right away, and I didn't want to have to stop in the middle of the party to run the credit card machine."

We all trooped into the back room, where Eula looked annoyed to see her artwork under a tarp and behind a Swiffer, but George waited patiently while Eula pulled out the three paintings and told him they were inspired by Cezanne, but with more veggies than fruit. George half listened while he examined the third canvas, which had an ornate gold frame complete with baroque carvings of birds, leaves, and trompe l'oeil swags. As Eula rattled on about her brushwork, George inspected the edges of the tiny third painting, and stepped back to stare at the canvas from a distance of several feet, then interrupted her.

"Eula, do you remember what was underneath your painting?" he asked. "Was it a landscape—maybe with a river?"

Eula thought for a moment and nodded.

"You know what, it was a landscape, but the colors were really dull," she said. "I got it for fifteen bucks at the flea market, which I thought was worth it since the frame is so nice."

"If it's okay with you, I'm going to borrow this for a few days and take it to New York with me tomorrow," George told her, carefully tucking the painting under his arm. "I'll call you in the morning to get you to sign some paperwork, since I'm going to need to remove some paint from the lower right hand corner of the canvas."

With that, George told Eula he thought her tomatoes had been painted on top of a small oil study by Honey Potts's favorite artist, Hasley Huntingdon-Mews, and that a similar tiny work by the same artist had sold the previous month for sixty thousand dollars.

GEORGE LEFT BY the back door with Eula's painting. Stunned, I went back out front and downed some peach punch while Eula wandered out glassy-eyed with shock.

When John showed up, I gave him the quick version of Eula's possible good fortune as Bootsie listened skeptically.

"George Fogle is wrong *a lot*," she told Eula. "I wouldn't get too excited if I were you."

"If you did suddenly get a massive amount of cash, you still want to sail around the world, though, right?" asked Holly hopefully.

"I guess so," said Eula. "Although I'm loving my new job at the *Gazette*! Did you see my story about Gianni's goat farm today?"

"Eula, once again, you missed the real story," Bootsie told her. "Gianni's goats aren't producing any goat cheese. He's been buying up chevre all over town, and repackaging it as his own."

"Uh-huh, sure," said Eula skeptically. "Bootsie, I know you're mad that we're competing for front-page stories now, but you don't have to make up lies."

"I'm not lying!" screamed Bootsie. "Gianni went behind his mafia investors' backs to start this goat cheese gig, and he's one of the secret owners of the Mega Wine Mart. He might be dead by next week if those goats don't start making some cheese!"

Eula stared at Bootsie for a minute, then doubled over laughing.

"You're hilarious!" Eula told her. "Well, I've gotta go. George said he's heading back to New York tonight, and who knows, maybe he'll call me with great news about my painting!" With that, she headed to her Miata and drove away.

"That girl is super annoying," observed Gerda.

"That's it," said Holly, downing her peach punch and picking up her handbag to leave. "I can't look at Eula in one more beige outfit. I'm done."

"You going to have her kidnapped?" asked Gerda. "I don't want to do anything too illegal, but maybe I could help."

"I'm still counting on the Powerball ticket to permanently remove Eula," Holly told her. "Right now, I'm calling Saks and having an entire wardrobe sent to her house tomorrow."

THE NEXT MORNING, I was just emerging from a ten-hour sleep of pure bliss when Bootsie called.

"Didn't you get my texts last night?" she demanded.

"I turned off my phone."

"There was an incident at Gianni's, and this time, it's serious!"

Bootsie had actually gone out to dinner with her own husband; she and Will had secured Table 11, which, she informed me, is well known among Gianni's regulars as being perfectly positioned mid-restaurant, with unobstructed views of both the bar and the dining room. Gianni and Abby hadn't arrived when she and Will were seated by the hostess, but had shown up several minutes later, with Gianni working the room and greeting customers for a few minutes, then sitting with Abby at a candlelit table back by the patio.

"They ordered Nonna Claudia's famous spaghetti alla chitarra, so I figured if Gianni was getting it, it must be the best thing on the menu," Bootsie told me. "I was waving down our waiter to ask for the same thing when I noticed the Binghams were seated up by the front window, and Gianni left Abby to go talk to them, which was weird, because who knew the Binghams were friends with Gianni?"

"That is odd," I agreed, heading for the bathroom to brush my teeth.

"So then the Binghams got into a testy conversation with Gianni, which isn't like them at all, and then Mr. Bingham said he was real confused by the papers Gianni sent over earlier that day . . . which apparently mentioned Mega Wine Mart instead of Maison de Booze."

"We should have known Gianni was involved." I sighed.

"From what I could hear, it sounded like the Binghams really *did* only agree to allow the Maison de Booze," Bootsie said. "That's why they were upset. Things got heated, and Gianni told them they should go outside and have some wine on the patio. So the three of them went out there, still arguing, and then I stopped trying to listen, because my spaghetti had just been served, and fresh pasta can't wait."

"Uh-huh," I said, carrying my phone downstairs to fire up the coffeemaker.

"Apparently, two guys in leather sport coats then showed up and the Binghams and Gianni left with them," Bootsie said. "In a town car. And they didn't come back."

I digested this for a minute. "Do you mean the two guys kidnapped them?"

"Um—probably?" said Bootsie. "I was eating, so I didn't see the incident."

"I thought you said you had Table 11 and that you were facing the whole restaurant and parking area! How did you miss a kidnapping?"

"You know how I am with pasta," admitted Bootsie. "I got distracted. But Abby saw the whole thing. She said it was totally peaceful and nonviolent, no guns or anything, so she waited twenty minutes, and finally gave up and went home.

"But the more I thought about it, there's no way Gianni would voluntarily leave a date with Abby," she said. "So maybe he's been abducted."

"You need to call Sophie," I said.

"THIS IS CLASSIC Jersey revenge," Sophie told me, Bootsie, and Gerda forty-five minutes later. We were in Sophie's pretty but empty living room. "Also, it sounds like Phil was involved, since he keeps asking about Mega Wine Mart."

"I can't believe Phil would kidnap Gianni and the Binghams," I said. "He seems so nice. Except for when he talks about Diana-Maria."

"Phil is nice, but you don't want to screw him over," Sophie told us. "Let me give him a call and see what's up."

She disappeared outside for a minute, talking animatedly on her cell phone.

"Phil's with the Binghams, and he said that now he knows they really are clueless," Sophie reported when she came back inside. "They told him they signed all the papers thinking it was going to be that Maison de Booze. All of this is some secret deal cooked up Gianni and my ex.

"The problem is that Phil and Sweet Freddie are supposed to get right of first refusal on any of Gianni's business deals, but Gianni and Barclay didn't tell Freddie about the Wine Mart. And," Sophie added, looking worried, "Sweet Freddie's behind the kidnapping."

"Sweet Freddie!" I shrieked, worried about the tipsy older couple. "The fingernail guy? The Binghams aren't cut out for dealing with tough guys."

"What if that happens to the Binghams!" screamed Bootsie. "There's not enough white zinfandel in the world to numb that kind of pain!"

"That was a one-time deal with the fingernails," Sophie told us, sitting down on the floor and drumming her manicure on the wood floor. "Once he did that, no one ever messed with Sweet Freddie again.

"Anyway, the Binghams are fine—a little confused, but Phil got them a few bottles of wine, and said they're being well taken care of in an undisclosed location," Sophie said. "The Binghams think they're on vacation, and they keep asking if there will be dancing later."

"Are they in A.C.?" asked Bootsie hopefully.

"I thought so at first, too," Sophie said, "but then I remembered Phil's favorite place to take people he kidnaps: Midnight Tony's Frog Creek Inn. It's real secluded.

"I know the security guy there, and I heard him greet Phil just now when we were talking on the phone," she added. "We need to head down there right now, because not only should we spring the Binghams, I heard another real familiar voice in the background—my ex, Barclay!"

Chapter 23

"Is Sweet Freddie at this Frog Creek place, too?" I asked once we had piled into Bootsie's car, which I assumed would be heading to the Bryn Mawr Police Station.

Now that I thought about it, I was pretty sure I'd once read a story about Sweet Freddie in *Time* magazine at the dentist's office, and it had not been a glowing portrayal. Sure, the guy was an avid consumer of candy, but his nickname was one meant ironically, since fingernails weren't the only thing Freddie was known to rip from victims when he was in a bad mood.

"I wouldn't worry too much. He barely ever kills anyone," Sophie reassured us.

"I'm not sure we're the best ones to solve a kidnapping!" I told her and Bootsie, noticing Bootsie had turned left toward the highway when she should have turned right toward town. "I mean, isn't this a problem for Walt? Or, you know, the FBI?"

"I promised Phil I wouldn't call anyone in law enforcement," Sophie said. "He thinks he can get this whole thing straightened out by 10 p.m."

"Great—we should probably stay home then!"

"Well." Sophie hesitated. "Sometimes Freddie doesn't make good on his word. But he loves me, so we should be fine if I'm there to smooth things over. Probably," she added.

"Walt's a police officer!" I protested. "Sophie, you've been away from dealing with guys like Phil and Freddie for a few years now. You're out of practice. And Bootsie's terrible in this kind of situation. She always goes off script. We'll all end somewhere deep in a defunct quarry!"

"Trust me," Sophie said confidently. "You can take the girl out of Jersey, but you can't take the Jersey out of the girl! I'll have the Binghams sprung by midnight."

"Count me in," said Bootsie.

"I help, too," said Gerda.

"Don't count me in!" I said, but Bootsie was already zooming up the on-ramp toward Jersey.

"If I was Gianni, though, I'd have headed back to L.A. before I got kidnapped," Sophie added thoughtfully. "Phil and Freddie really hate him."

MIDNIGHT TONY'S FROG Creek Inn was down a secluded road just past Midnight Tony's restaurant. The setting would have been adorable, if we hadn't been dealing with a kidnapping. There was a boathouse and a pretty little wooden bridge over what I guessed was the eponymous creek, which indeed was filled with the loud croaking of five-pound bullfrogs in an amorous summer mood.

The building was a two-story mansion evoking Charleston or Savannah, with waterfront terraces and wide glass doors that afforded a view of a swanky, glitzy lobby.

Purple spotlights framed the front portico, and electronic

music pulsated, which added to the party vibe . . . crystal and gold chandeliers sparkled inside the front doors, and the concierge desk was made of purple quilted leather . . . it all looked oddly familiar to me.

Then it clicked.

"Sophie, this place looks like a giant version of your old house when you were married to Barclay!" I whispered.

"We had the same designer come out to Pennsylvania and go crazy with crystals and the purple marble. Which Joe then ripped out." She paused, looking sad for a minute. "To be honest, it was a little too much purple for Pennsylvania, but that doesn't mean I won't do something similar just to spite Joe if I have to."

"Well, anyway, the vibe is really fun," I said.

"I would not call it fun, having to dust of all those lights, and replace the bulbs probably every day, creating a ton of discarded landfill light bulbs," Gerda said, casting a critical eye skyward. "Ton of work and waste of not only energy, but think of the Windex they gotta use. This place make no sense."

"I can't let you in," said Junior, Sophie's security guard/doorman buddy when we got to the little bridge. He pulled a regretful face. "Boss's orders." He leaned in to whisper. "But I can tell you that your ex-husband's here."

"Barclay?" said Sophie. "We're still married, by the way! What's he doing here?"

"He showed up about thirty minutes ago, with Mr. LaMonte's girlfriend Diana-Maria," Junior told her. "And Mr. LaMonte is real mad!"

Sophie's face froze.

"Were my ex and Diana-Maria, like, together romantically?" she said.

"Looked like it," Junior said regretfully. "I'm real sorry."

"Not as sorry as he's gonna be," shouted Sophie, who, though she's been dating Joe for more than a year, has always maintained that Barclay shouldn't be allowed to see other women—to make up for all the ones he saw during their marriage.

"Anyway," said Junior, looking uncomfortable, "I'm not allowed to let anyone into the hotel today. There's some kind of big meeting going on, and it's private."

He indicated the closed gate. "Sorry, Mrs. Shields," he said as Sophie waved a handful of twenties at him. "I'd let ya in, but my wife had a baby last month, and if I get fired, or if Phil kills me, I'll feel real guilty about letting my family down."

BOOTSIE DROVE BACK down the lane, now shrouded in darkness, took a left into a grove of pine trees, then turned off the engine.

"Lucky for us, I've been too busy to unpack the car since I got back from Maine," she said. "I only wish Will hadn't gotten the kayaks off the roof, but I might have something even better." She popped open the trunk and grabbed two bundles of yellow nylon and various gadgets including foot pumps, bungee cords, and paddles.

"You got two of the twelve-foot Adventurer Inflatable paddleboards?" asked Gerda, impressed. "I help you inflate."

In four minutes flat, Bootsie and Gerda had inflated and were paddling the yellow nylon boards across Frog Creek, while Sophie and I perched precariously on the watercraft.

"You think there are snakes in this river?" asked Gerda. "Sophie, if I were you, I'd keep your feet out of water. Looks snakey to me."

Once across the creek, it was easy to find the Binghams, since their hotel suite was right on the water, and they were waving from their terrace. They greeted us enthusiastically, and we trooped inside a large, tasteful suite, where Lobster Phil, Gianni, and a turtlelike man who could only be Sweet Freddie awaited.

"Freddie, hiya!" said Sophie, and the little man broke a smile.

"Sophie, you got gumption. You take up rafting or something since I last saw ya?"

"I really wanted to see you and tell you in person that these two"—here, she pointed at the Binghams—"are innocent. Ya can let them go," she added in a whisper, "and they probably won't remember this happened by tomorrow."

"These gentlemen have been so nice," said Mrs. Bingham. "I mean, they went out last night and got us a case of our favorite white zinfandel, and just look at this Brie and cracker tray." She smiled at Lobster Phil. "I'm still not sure which one of you is Barry Tutto, but this has been a real hoot."

"It's probably a fake name! And there might not even be a Maison de Booze," Bootsie told her. "There's been a lot of double-dealing, Mrs. Bingham."

The Binghams looked at Gianni with an expression in which tipsiness and hurt were commingled.

"You said the town would *love* Maison de Booze," Mr. Bingham said.

"They would," Bootsie said, "except that it'll be torn down in eight weeks for a superstore."

"So you weren't joking?" said Mr. Bingham. "And who's Barry Tutto? Is it you?" he asked Sweet Freddie.

Sweet Freddie gave a death glare to Gianni. "You explain," he ordered the chef.

"A little joke," said Gianni. "*Bere tutto* means drink up in Italian. Cute little name for a development partnership that Barclay and I put together!"

Sweet Freddie looked annoyed. "I told you I'd kill you if you tried to open a liquor business without giving me a cut," he informed Gianni. "And I didn't get a phone call about either a Maison de Whatever, or a Mega Wine Mart."

"This was naughty of you," Mrs. Bingham said to Gianni, looking disappointed.

"Hey, I tried, not everything always work out, even for Gianni!" said Gianni, shrugging. "I know people like to get drunk, I figure we open the little wine store and Sweet Freddie here never know about it. Then I was gonna ask you about the megastore!" he told the imposing little man in front of him.

"But Gianni don't need this aggravation. I give up on megastore!" he added.

"It's not giving up when I told you I'd kill you. And here's another piece of info: If you go behind my back, I'll rip off your earlobes and mail them back to you in a birthday card," Freddie announced.

"Sure, whatever you say!" said Gianni. He grabbed his leather jacket and took his phone back from Lobster Phil. "I gonna get your organic cheese to you, Freddie, and we gonna make a ton of money from my restaurants. Don't worry!"

"The goat farm is under new management—me," Freddie returned. "But I want you to make sure the herd starts producing a ton of cheese, pronto."

"Sure, okay," said Gianni. "Then I gotta get back to filming *The Angry Chef*. I save best table for you, you come visit in California and we have a great time!" Gianni said.

"I better," said Freddie.

"I still can't figure out who stabbed Gianni last week," mused Bootsie. "So many people want to kill him."

"Ya don't know?" said Lobster Phil. "I bribed a guy from The Trendy Tent. I heard Gianni had a fling with Diana-Maria, and I was upset."

"I never sleep with her!" Gianni yelled. "I try to, but your girlfriend turn me down. You got a guy to stab me for no reason!"

"Consider it a warning," Phil told him.

"I have a question for you, Mr., um, Sweet Freddie," said Bootsie. "We have a friend, Holly Jones, who'd like to go ahead and open the wine store in the old garden shack. I was thinking of investing in it, too, if that's okay with you."

Sweet Freddie cast an appraising eye at Bootsie.

"How many square feet?" he asked.

"About twenty-five hundred," she told him. "We'd do mostly wine, and obviously there'd be a cheese section. No hard liquor, and closed Sundays, with free tastings Tuesdays and Thursdays."

Lobster Phil was nodding. "The area's real beautiful, Freddie. Shame to see someone else like Sophie's ex or this guy"—here, he indicated Gianni, who was texting and shrugged, unabashed—"ruin the trees and forest there. A small shop would be nice."

Freddie nodded, reaching out to shake first Bootsie's hand.

"I can see you know how to run a no-bullshit operation!" he told her approvingly. "I had an aunt reminds me of you. I like tall girls."

"This one can eat like a dockhand, too!" Sophie told Freddie. "You should see her around a lasagna."

"Good for you," said Freddie. "Call me if you come to Vegas. I approve of your wine store. Good luck!"

"I steer paddleboards back across the river," Gerda said. "Probably better if you meet me at car with these oldies," she said, indicating the Binghams.

"We'll have Junior drive you across the bridge," Phil agreed.

"I just need one more quick favor," Sophie pouted. "My ex and Diana-Maria are in the Waterside Suite, and I have reason to believe he has seventeen pairs of my Gucci sandals with him. Diana-Maria also wears a size five and a half, plus Barclay has a weird thing for ladies' shoes," she added by way of explanation. "Anyway, could I grab 'em back while he's still out at dinner?"

"He stole your shoes? That's real disturbing," Freddie said. He walked us down the hallway a few yards, and with a master key opened the door to a lavish suite with river views.

"My sandals!" screamed Sophie, running toward a display of glittery platforms that had been arranged on a fireplace mantel. "Dang it, I forgot to bring a tote bag, and my Guccis are real delicate."

"No problem," Bootsie told her, and pulled a blue nylon tube out of her pocket. She yanked a strap, and the L.L. Bean packable sink popped into shape. "This sink has twenty-five-liter capacity, so seventeen pairs of shoes are gonna be a perfect fit."

Chapter 24

WE WERE IN Bootsie's SUV on the way home from A.C. when my phone dinged with a text from Holly. "The Colketts are at my house, and they have news. Officer Walt's coming over, and you need to get here ASAP."

"Maybe they did take the painting! Will we ever know where *Heifer* was for the last week?" Bootsie wondered. "And is it like the proverbial tree that fell in the forest, if that's the phrase I'm looking for? On a cosmic level, do we need to know where it is?"

"Maybe there is connection between the painting and the Wine Mart," offered Gerda.

"We got the Binghams back, and it looks like the Wine Mart is kaput, so maybe we should leave well enough alone," I suggested.

"Do you think, um, Louis Pasteur left well enough alone? Or George Washington or FDR or for that matter, L.L. Bean?" Bootsie demanded.

"I hear you," Sophie piped up. "I mean, think of Lady Gaga. Who else would have worn a dress entirely constructed of meat? Some people were born to push the envelope!"

"How is meat dress pertinent to finding a painting?" asked Gerda.

"It's a metaphor," said Bootsie. "Anyway, I predict within a week, my investigative skills will uncover the exact movements of *Heifer in Tomato Patch*."

AFTER WE DROPPED the Binghams at their house, we headed to Holly's patio, lit by lanterns and with Brazilian music emanating from hidden speakers. The Colketts faced Officer Walt with tipsy but determined forthrightness.

"We wanted to come clean before we head back to Beverly Hills," said Tom. "I don't think we did anything that's too illegal," he added hopefully.

"It was all kind of a joke," said Tim, "brought on by too much time with Eula bossing us around at that Tomato Party. And maybe one too many Bloody Marys. But just to be clear, we didn't steal *Heifer in Tomato Patch*. However, we did *see* it after it was pilfered."

"This was all on the same night it went missing—the night Gianni showed up at the club and got stabbed," his business partner explained. "We were totally flustered, and went into the men's locker room to sneak a cigarette when I happened to look up and notice *Heifer* hanging over the laundry bin. We knew it was the original, because for a cow painting, it was really special. I mean, the thing glowed.

"We didn't say anything," Tom continued apologetically, "figuring it was right there for everyone to see, and you'd find it in, like, fifteen minutes. But the next morning, *Heifer* was still missing, and we were going to tell you it was in the locker room. But when we got to the country club, it was gone and replaced by a portrait of one of the past club presidents from, like, 1920, so we kept our mouths shut."

"Then a couple days ago, we were at the storage locker we rent out by the highway, because we remembered we had some amazing chairs that once might have belonged to Bette Davis and are super-sexy, clubby numbers in black lacquer that would be perfect for the foyer at Gianni's place in L.A.," Tim said.

"And while we were at our storage space, we found a couple of kitschy paintings we bought from the guy who sells corndogs out at Stoltzfus's Flea Market," he continued. "We thought they'd be perfect for a client with a sense of humor who wanted, like, a tavern in their paneled basement or something. Anyway, one of them was an identical copy of *Heifer in Tomato Patch*. We snuck over to the country club and hung it up in the Camellia Room. It was a hoot!"

"We also found a fake Picasso that we boxed up and dropped at the Pack-N-Ship to be delivered to Gianni at the Beverly Hills restaurant," Tom said. "We mail him stuff anonymously all the time."

"Last month we sent him a leather toilet seat and a case of Spam," Tim said. "Seeing him get mad helps when you're working twenty-two-hour days. Anyway, then I realized I always kind of liked that Picasso fake. So on Monday morning, we stopped back at the Pack-N-Ship, and while Tom distracted Leena at the front counter, I went around back and stole our painting back from her storeroom. Which probably isn't a crime—right?"

"Uh-huh," said Walt, who'd given up on taking notes. His face registered surprise and consternation. "So you saw the real *Heifer* painting at the club on the night it went missing. But then it was gone the next morning, and you never saw it again."

"Exactly," said Tom, jumping up. "And if it's okay, we've got Uber waiting again outside and heading right to the airport. We need to be back at Gianni's new restaurant at eight tomorrow morning. This has been fun!"

Chapter 25

GERDA'S PILATES STUDIO launched the following Monday, and classes immediately sold out for the next two months. Part two of the Tomato Show opened the same afternoon, and Mrs. Potts gave her lecture about tomatoes, pastoral art, and Hasley Huntingdon-Mews. Unfortunately, her prized painting was still missing, since no one had been able to trace its movements after the Colketts had seen it in the men's locker room. As for Eula Morris, all week she'd been avoiding Bootsie, who'd wanted to grill Eula about the copy of *Heifer* the Colketts had bought at Stoltzfus's.

"That speech was real boring," Sophie announced after Mrs. Potts wound up her forty-five-minute monologue. "But I'm happy for Mrs. Potts. Let's go check out these veggies!"

Rows of white tables groaned under robust, carefully manicured plants from which dangled every size, shape, and color of tomato. I looked at Beefsteaks, Mortgage Lifters, Mr. Stripeys, and Yellow Pears, which all looked delicious, but left me wondering— were they worth making secret trips to a Jersey greenhouse?

Just then, I saw Lilly Merriwether give Bootsie a hug, then head in the direction of the parking lot.

"Lilly's gone again!" Bootsie told me four seconds later. "Heading back to Connecticut. She and her boyfriend are back together."

"Great!" I said, barely restraining a fist pump and a jig. I could breathe again, safe in the knowledge that Lilly and her Lacoste tennis outfits would be ruining the days of other women farther up the East Coast, and that I could go to the Pub and the grocery store without bracing myself for sightings of her willowy blond form.

I paused to look at a blue ribbon placed on a plant bursting with neat orange tomatoes. "First Prize for Sun Golds: Eula Morris."

"Guess what!" shrieked Eula, arriving at the table and apparently out of hiding. "That painting George saw at your shop, Kristin, *is* a small Huntingdon-Mews. And it's worth, like, fifty thousand dollars! George just called me. They had to ship it to England to some expert there, and they just got word!"

I was floored. I'd almost forgotten about Eula's possible windfall from the canvas upon which she'd painted her own tomato still life. Bootsie's mouth fell open, and Holly did an eye roll and left to go talk to the Binghams about their Sweet 100s, which had come in second place.

"I'm rich!" said Eula, then picked up her tiny feet and did a happy dance.

"Not so fast—you should split that money with Kristin," Bootsie told Eula. "You never would have found out the painting was worth anything if she hadn't offered to sell it at The Striped Awning. You would have sold your crappy tomato painting at Stoltzfus's for seventy-five dollars if Kristin hadn't been willing to take it on in her store."

"No, it's fine," I said, embarrassed. "The painting belongs to Eula. I was only going to take ten percent commission if it sold at the shop."

"You could give her ten percent, Eula," Sophie suggested. "That would be the least ya can do for Kristin, and what's a measly five grand when you'll still be getting, like, forty-five thousand dollars?"

I could see Eula wrestling in her mind about the ten percent. She's not all that good at hiding her emotions, and her face registered dismay, confusion, a twinge of guilt, and greed.

"Also, Eula, if you don't hand over Kristin's ten percent, I'll tell the tomato committee you grew your Early Girls in New Jersey, and they'll strip you of your first place ribbon," Bootsie said, making a bomb-detonating hand gesture. "Boom! Does that help you make up your mind?"

Eula's expression changed instantly, adopting instant regret.

"That sounds fair," she said. "It's gonna take a month to get the canvas restored, and then George said he'll put it in an auction in early September. I'll keep you posted."

"Thank you so much!" I told her, genuinely elated. Five grand would enable me to pay off almost all my bills, catch up on rent on The Striped Awning, and hopefully cut back my hours at the Pack-N-Ship to every other weekend.

"By the way," said Eula with a shrug, "now that I'm getting this huge windfall of cash, and we're being all honest here, you know that fake *Heifer in Tomato Patch* that was returned to the club last week? I *did* paint it."

"I knew it!" yelled Bootsie.

"I was scared to admit it to Walt," Eula told us. "I didn't want him to think I'd stolen the original. And I honestly don't know how my copy got to the club. I sold it at Stoltzfus's last summer, and I painted it more than a year ago after I took a garden club tour at Mrs. Potts's place and was able to sneak a few pics of it.

"Well, I better go get on my computer and start planning how to spend all this cash!" Eula added, picking up a couple of tomato plants and the accompanying blue ribbons. Just as she tripped happily up the porch steps, a giant vegetable flew down from the top floor of the club and squashed onto Eula's head.

"It was only a four-pounder," said Holly. "We got it overnighted from a farmer in Wisconsin who won the state fair this year. That was still pretty awesome though."

"THAT PAINTING CASH is enough to get rid of Eula for a few months," said Holly five minutes later, after Eula had stormed out, covered in tomato. "She'll go on a great vacation somewhere, but it's not enough for that cruise." She sighed tragically. "If I know Eula, she'll rent a house in Hilton Head or Barbados, blow through the money, and be back in three months."

"At least we'll be Eula-free for most of the fall," I said, looking around the tomato exhibits, which had a festive air. I couldn't help noticing that the event was your basic country-club festivity—very pretty, with white tablecloths and a few bunches of hydrangeas on the tables, and Abby the waitress passing around pigs in a blanket.

The club was back to normal!

"Where are Gianni's sous-chefs?" I asked Holly. "And why isn't the customized smoker turning out short ribs that have been marinated for forty-eight hours and gently massaged?"

"Gianni flew back to Los Angeles last night, and he told his staff to go back to his restaurant," Holly said. "Skipper is back in the kitchen. The Colketts left, too."

"Are you going to tell the committee about Eula's secret greenhouse?" I asked Bootsie.

"I decided to keep that piece of information, and the photos, which are date- and time-stamped, to myself—for now," Bootsie said, with a slightly evil smile. "You never know when we're going to need a favor from Eula."

"Speaking of Eula," said Holly, "that Powerball drawing is tonight, and I have a very strong feeling we're going to win. Does anyone know how much the jackpot's up to this week? Is it enough to get rid of Eula permanently?"

"Are you gonna try to win Powerball and then hire someone to take out Eula?" breathed Sophie. "Because that can backfire. Barclay told me that professional hit men always come back for more money!"

At this, Holly went to the bar, got some water, and popped three aspirin, while I explained quickly to Sophie that the plan was to make Eula's dream vacation happen—not have her killed.

"The mega-jackpot's up to $256 million, because no one's won for like two months," Bootsie told me, after doing some quick iPhone Googling. "They keep putting all the cash back into the award pool, so it's huge for tomorrow's drawing."

"Two hundred fifty-six million," echoed Sophie, elated. "That would be so awesome! If I won Powerball, I'd tell Barclay to go screw himself and buy those poor goats from Gianni and Sweet Freddie! I'm gonna stop at the deli after this and get, like, five tickets for myself!"

"Uh-huh," said Bootsie skeptically. "So if you win, you're going to spend a quarter of a billion dollars on goat cheese?"

"What else?" asked Sophie. "I mean, I'd give some to charity, too, and take care of my relatives in Jersey, plus I'd probably hit Neiman's, but mostly I keep thinking about those little goats."

"Sounds like work," said Bootsie. "Plus wouldn't you have to make good on Gianni's deal to provide organic goat cheese to a bunch of restaurants in Las Vegas?"

"I've been thinking about that," said Sophie. "Those Amish guys, the Stoltzfuses, we met out at Gianni's place are super-nice. I think they could do their own deal with Sweet Freddie and Lobster Phil, and make it a real legit business. It would be good for everyone! The farmers would make beaucoup cash, and Phil and Freddie might learn a few lessons about respectable business-people who will never let them down, overcharge them, or dump them feet-first in Absecon Bay!"

"I guess," said Bootsie doubtfully.

"See you gals later!" Sophie sang out, grabbing her handbag and heading for the club parking lot. "It's Powerball time and I gotta pick all my lucky numbers!"

BY EIGHT THAT night, we were all at the Bryn Mawr Pub, where we ordered the one-hundred-wing bucket and pitchers of beer. John had joined us, and we were catching him up on Eula's fifty-thousand-dollar pentimento painting, plus the well-aimed giant tomato that Joe had neatly dropped from a third-floor window.

"Hey, isn't that Abby from the club?" Bootsie asked, pointing a half-eaten wing in the direction of the dartboard in the back room. "Hey, Abby, over here!" she shouted, and Abby waved and walked to the front of the bar to squeeze into our booth next to Bootsie.

"Is that your boyfriend from college?" Sophie asked her, nodding toward a tall blond guy in cargo shorts and a polo. "'Cause he's real cute."

"Yup." Abby nodded proudly. "He, um, doesn't know anything about those couple of dates I had with Gianni, so if you could not mention it, I'd really appreciate it." She looked nervous for a few seconds, gulped some beer, and then spoke up again.

"There's another thing I wanted to tell you guys, if you can promise you won't tell Officer Walt or Eula Morris or Mrs. Potts," she whispered. "I'm terrified of Mrs. P.! I can barely serve her lunch without my hands shaking!"

"Is it something bad about Eula Morris?" Holly asked hopefully. "We're excellent at keeping secrets, by the way. You can tell us anything."

"Great!" said Abby, relieved. "It's not about Eula, though. It's about that painting that went missing."

"WHAT HAPPENED WAS that the day when the Colketts were there setting up the tent for the big Tomato Show party and Eula was bossing everyone around, me and Stacy, the lunchtime waitress, got really tired of it," Abby told us.

"Setting up the bar in the tent took forever, and then we had to help the Colketts arrange about eight thousand hydrangeas on the porch, and Eula kept making us reposition those rented sofas from The Trendy Tent, which weighed a ton! So Stacy and I each had four shots of tequila out in the tent when we were setting up the margarita machine, because finally Eula and the Colketts went inside to have lunch." She looked embarrassed at this. "Which I feel real bad about.

"We like you and the Colketts, though!" Abby told Holly. "Anyway, after the tequila shots, we heard Mrs. Potts make them rehang her painting for, like, the twelfth time, Stacy and I snuck into the Camellia Room, and—this seemed like a good idea, but we were honestly really drunk—we took the painting of the cow and hung it in the men's locker room over the trash can!

"There was a painting of an old guy there, so there were two picture hooks already on the wall, and we replaced it with the *Heifer* thingy."

We all stared at Abby.

"So the Colketts *did* see *Heifer in Tomato Patch* in the men's locker room," said Holly. "Did you move it again?"

"No!" whispered Abby. "Because when we sobered up later that night, when Officer Walt arrived and we realized this was a major fuckup, we went into the locker room, and it was gone!"

"Excuse me," said a wavy-haired guy at the bar, turning around to face our table. "Remember me? I'm Randy, Gianni's cameraman. I think I have something to add to this story.

"I'm real sorry, but I was in a seriously bad mood when Gianni and I got to that country club on that Thursday," the guy said, sipping his Corona. "I snuck out to that party tent, too, and drank everything I could get my hands on.

"Then when I heard the ruckus about a missing painting, I figured I could frame Gianni!"

Randy said he'd gone into locker room to use the bathroom and had seen a big framed painting that even in his drunken state he knew had to be *Heifer.*

Without much thought, he grabbed the painting and stuck it in the back of his rented car with his camera equipment, then drove to Ristorante Gianni to do some more drinking. Later that night, when Gianni was at the emergency room and the staff were busy with the dinner service, he'd stealthily gone in via Gianni's delivery entrance and hung the painting—where else—on a convenient hook in the men's room. A scene of ancient Rome that had been displayed there he'd stuck in his rental car, where it still resided.

"I feel kinda bad about this," Randy admitted. "I figured someone would notice the fancy painting in Gianni's restaurant's bathroom—but I guess no one has!"

Randy jumped up. "Well, I'm headed to the airport—see ya. The Food Network wants me to film the return of Nonna Claudia to L.A. They're doubling her pay to come back. They love her!"

"I always thought you made up these stories about the stuff that happens whenever I leave town," John told me, shaking his head as he sipped his beer.

As Randy left, Eula arrived, her face in complete shock.

"Remember how I told you someone dropped off ten Powerball tickets in my mailbox last week?" she asked Bootsie.

"Of course I remember," said Bootsie. "Not that I'd know anything about who bought them for you," she amended.

"Well—I won!" screamed Eula, jumping up and down in front of the bar. "I won Powerball!"

The bar erupted into applause, except for Holly and Joe, who were frozen in their seats, their faces in complete shock.

"The Lotto Commission already announced that only five winning tickets were sold," Eula sang out. "I'm gonna get, like, $50 million! I can finally take that round-the-world cruise!"

THIRTY MINUTES LATER, Eula left to start researching her cruise, and Holly and Joe were able to move their lips again.

"I thought that's what you wanted," Sophie said to Joe. "To send that girl on vacation."

"I did," said Joe. "I just didn't think through the fact that I'll be arranging dishtowels for Adelia Earle next week while Eula's doing a back flip into the Mediterranean."

"Cheer up, Honey Bunny!" Sophie told him. "I got some Powerball tickets, too! They're right here in my purse." She pulled out some slips of paper and examined them, looking bewildered.

"These are something else—but I pointed at Powerball. At least, I think I did. The guy at the deli told me to pick five numbers and I paid him twenty dollars."

"You bought the Pick 5," Bootsie told her, inspecting the tickets Sophie had produced. "That's different. I'll check the winning numbers for you."

While Bootsie did some quick research on her phone, Sophie told us that there'd been a huge breakthrough on her divorce deal. It seemed that Freddie and Lobster Phil had sat down with Barclay over drinks in Atlantic City, and suggested that for both his and Sophie's sake, they thought he should fork over half his worldly goods and move on.

"Phil and Freddie told Barclay that he should look for a new wife now—before he starts gaining weight again!" Sophie told us. "It's only a matter of time. And they said that Joe and I make a great couple!"

"They did?" said Joe, surprised. "Those two goombahs—I mean, those guys—are in favor of you and me as a couple?"

"Sophie," said Bootsie, looking up from her phone, "this is unbelievable. You got the Pick 5! You won two hundred and fifty thousand dollars—tax free!"

TRUE TO HER word, Sophie made Gianni an offer for his goat farm the next morning, which he took, even though he complained about the fifteen thousand dollars he'd already spent on the cheese kitchen.

"I can tell Gianni's really glad he's back in L.A.," Sophie said when we met for lunch at the country club the next day. Things were back to normal here, and a blissful summer breeze floated over the wide porch. At neighboring tables, Binghams were sipping white zinfandel, Mrs. Potts was eating fried oysters with Mike Woodford, and Abby was cheerfully bringing out drinks to a group of elderly golfers

"I don't know anything about goats, but I'm gonna have those nice Amish guys run the place, and my Honey Bunny and I can go out there on weekends and, like, have special time alone in nature!" Sophie said, giving Joe a loving pat on the arm.

"That is, as soon as I get a satellite disk, wi-fi, and one of those really cool new Williams-Sonoma cappuccino machines installed," she added. "And a pool. I mean, it's a little rustic out there right now."

"I think you're going to be really good at goat farming, Sophie," said John, who was sitting next to me, holding my hand. He gave my fingers a little squeeze. "The Stoltzfuses will do a great job running the place for you. I was out there yesterday, and the goats are thriving."

"It's real handy that Kristin's dating a vet!" Sophie told him gratefully. "Especially one as handsome as you."

Joe looked nervous about the goat farm idea, and flagged down Abby for another drink.

"And Gerda's got the name for her Pilates studio," Sophie told us. "Tell them, Gerda."

"I'm gonna call it Gerda's Bust Your Ass Gym," announced the eponymous owner.

"That says it all," agreed Bootsie, who'd arrived just behind them.

"Everyone in town is going to be there!" Holly promised. "Especially when they hear that I'm going to pay for Ursula to give free aromatherapy neck massages after every class for the first two months."

"Thank you," said Gerda, looking pleased.

"It's the least I can do when you singlehandedly took down Gianni, thanks to your new leopard pumps," Holly told her sweetly.

"Also," Holly told me, "I can't face peach punch ever again. I got you a margarita machine for your store, and Howard and I are sponsoring Tequila Tuesdays at The Striped Awning for the rest of the summer."

This sounded amazing! Just then, John excused himself and got up from our table. "I'm meeting Mrs. Potts and Mike Woodford to talk over some new breeding trends for their cows," he told me. "Would you like to join us?"

"No, thanks," I said hastily.

"I'll call you later," he said. "We can barbecue tonight."

Perfect! I thought. A breezy summer night with my boyfriend, whose ex-wife was back where she belonged in Connecticut. Things were totally going my way! I would soon be five thousand dollars richer, since Eula could now definitely afford to cut me my ten percent of her painting sale. Plus Joe had helped me with a great new look at The Striped Awning, and the town was seemingly free of mafia types as well as Gianni.

I stole a furtive look at Mike Woodford's tanned arms as he gave John a handshake and they all sat down together. Gosh, Mike looked good, I thought . . . and this town is really small . . . I need to get Mike one hundred percent out of my system. I should really meditate every morning until I've completely forgotten about Mike Woodford . . .

"Don't you have something to give to Sophie?" Holly prompted Joe, interrupting my thoughts.

Joe nervously pulled a small white box from his pocket, and Sophie's eyes widened in shock as he popped open the lid.

"Sophie," he said, "I'd love to marry you one day, but in the meantime, would you like to be preengaged, as signified by this amethyst once worn by Lady Gaga on the Cheek-to-Cheek Tour with Tony Bennett?" He wiped his brow nervously.

"Abso-freakin'-lutely!" shrieked Sophie, jumping into his arms.

About the Author

AMY KORMAN is the author of *Killer WASPs, Killer Getaway,* and *Frommer's Philadelphia and the Amish Country,* and is a former senior editor and staff writer for *Philadelphia Magazine.* She has written for *Town & Country, House Beautiful, Men's Health,* and *Cosmopolitan.* She lives in Pennsylvania with her family and their basset hound, Murphy.

Discover great authors, exclusive offers, and more at hc.com.